The Verbal Squatter
A Collection of South African Short Stories

Darrell Cuthbert

ISBN: 978-0620470667

Front cover photograph courtesy of:

StG Studios – Cape Town
www.stgstudios.co.za
+27 83 978 3143

Other artwork & designs by the author.

Author's Note: Why the Verbal Squatter?

A squatter is one who takes possession of a place not his own, then settles and makes his home there. Sadly squatting has become an increasingly common phenomenon in South Africa in recent times, due to economic hardship, unemployment and increased urbanisation. Settlements of shacks are to be seen near many suburbs as people seek to make a home for themselves, however rudimentary.

Without making light of the suffering of the inhabitants, driving past one such settlement en route to work everyday gave me a useful analogy in a rare flash of coherent thought.

I usually find inspiration for fictional stories in somebody else's life, or an event around me. So in a sense I take someone else's story and squat on it, grabbing the original territory and building on it as I choose with words and sentences instead of wood and metal.

My hope is that you enjoy reading these stories as much as I did writing them.

Note: Translations of local / slang terms appearing in italics can be found in the glossary at the back of the book.

Contents

The Two-Second Smile

Thabo walked down the line of cars waiting at the traffic light, trying to make eye contact with the drivers.

He found that he sold more newspapers if he could somehow connect with his potential customers. If they returned his glance he gave them one of his cheerful two-second smiles while allowing his eyes to drop towards the front-page headlines.

If the occupant of the car followed his gaze downwards he would move closer to the window to give them a better look at the news of the day. If he got this far he usually made a sale.

If they did not respond within the two seconds he moved on. He could not waste time on people who dithered. The light would change to green soon and the cars would move away to be replaced by a fresh batch of prospects.

There was not a lot of money to be made this way but it was better than begging. At least he had something to take home at the end of the day with which to buy food.

Every day he stood like this in the traffic, from the beginning of the morning rush hour to the end of the evening one.

It was that time now as the traffic began to thin out

and the noise reduced. He decided that there were unlikely to be more sales today. With sagging shoulders he packed up his remaining newspapers, retrieved his jacket from under a shrub on the traffic island and started walking.

He travelled six blocks to the rank where he would find a minibus taxi headed for the black townships south of the city. Once the taxi was squeezed full to the point of being slightly overloaded the driver set off. Thabo had been fortunate enough to be amongst the first to board and reserve a seat by the window. He enjoyed looking out at the houses and dreaming.

The taxi passed through several upmarket suburbs then lumbered down an on-ramp and joined the M1 South. The homes of the upper middle class were still visible standing distantly off to either side but they now had a detached feel. Thabo turned his attention instead to studying the traffic passing by.

The freeway snaked out into a more commercial area and became the top level of a triple-decker section, a scalpel cut through the heart of the city. From his vantage point Thabo gazed out into this blackened and diseased heart.

The dirty, broken windows and peeling paintwork bore silent witness to the inner city decay from which Johannesburg in common with many of its cousins on the continent suffered.

This imposing, if rather decrepit, view failed to impress the other occupants of the vehicle. Mostly they wore a tired, jaded look - induced by early mornings and long hours of work and travel.

The taxi stopped outside the imposing Chris Hani

Baragwanath Hospital (Bara to locals). Thabo climbed out and started the long walk home. As he walked the familiar sights and smells of Soweto surrounded him.

He instinctively placed his hand in his pocket over his wallet when passing a group of Tsotsis on the opposite street corner.

The smell of roasted meat hung on the breeze, teasing his hungry nostrils as he approached another street corner. A local woman cooked whole sheep head over an open fire for sale to passers by. This dish was often referred to as Smiley, because of the way the sheep's lips curled back during the cooking process, giving the impression that the lifeless head was grinning at you.

This was just one example of the quirky sense of humour of the townships, referring to chickens feet (another popular local dish), as Runaways was another.

Finally, tired and weary, Thabo arrived outside his home. As he passed through the gate the sun, looking equally tired and weary through the smog, was just touching the western horizon. Thankfully it was still summer. In the winter the last stretch would have to be walked in the dark, vastly increasing the chances of being robbed of the day's earnings.

Walking up to the door of the house Thabo could hear the metallic clanking of a spoon against the side of an aluminium pot and the children playing inside. He unlocked the door and let himself in, the familiar smell of burnt paraffin welcoming him. The children were not far behind in adding their welcomes, shrieking and jumping into his arms.

Sonto turned from the paraffin stove over which she had been working to greet him. Thabo smiled as the aroma of supper filtered through the air to his nostrils. *Pap* and chicken stew, his favourite.

Sonto had received her pay on Friday, hence the luxury of meat in the pot. Later in the month it would be back to pap and gravy with a few meaty bones thrown in for taste, or *umngqusho* (samp and beans) flavoured with chilli or onion.

Between Sonto's wages as a maid in one of the predominantly white suburbs and whatever Thabo made selling newspapers, they just managed to scrape by.

Sonto had by now finished dishing up the food onto four chipped enamel-coated tin plates. Holding hands the family agreed with Thabo as he offered up a prayer of thanks for the meal. They ate sitting on the worn and patched lounge suite that was given to them by Sonto's employers when they bought a new one a few years before.

The sounds of eating were accompanied by music from the cheap battery powered radio standing on a crude shelf in a corner of the small room. Television was a luxury beyond their reach. Besides the house had only two electrical outlets, one in the kitchen and one in the bedroom.

Likewise there were only three cold-water taps in the house, one in the kitchen and two in the bathroom. The kitchen area consisted of a counter running along one wall of the living area, with a small sink at one end.

This living room together with the small bedroom and even smaller bathroom made up the three rooms of the house. It wasn't much but they weren't complaining. They were far better off than some of their relatives and friends who lived in shacks made of cardboard, corrugated iron and whatever other makeshift building materials they could lay their hands on.

Supper was over and while Sonto washed the dishes Thabo took the opportunity to get Sipho and Disego to show him what they had learnt in school that day. This was the only time he had available to spend alone with the children. With him having to leave home very early in the morning and only return home in the evening, Thabo was not able to spend as much time with his son

and daughter as he would have liked, though he did try to catch up on the weekends.

While the children went to the bathroom to wash up and get ready for bed, he pulled out the foam mattresses from behind the couch and arranged them in the middle of the living room floor. Sonto came through from the bedroom with an armload of blankets and sheets Together they made up the makeshift beds as carefully as they could.

After having settled the little ones down for the night, Thabo spent a few minutes sitting in the doorway on the top step listening to the night sounds. He allowed himself to dream slightly of what it would be like to live in the suburbs, with a bedroom for each of the children and a large one for Sonto and himself to share. He fantasised about having a car in a garage like those he had seen in the suburbs. Most of those garages were larger than his house.

These thoughts stirred him from his seat and propelled him through to the bedroom. There he took out his books to study for an hour or so until he was too tired to concentrate. Sonto's employers had kindly agreed to lend them the money to allow Thabo to enrol in a correspondence college and deduct it from her salary in small amounts.

He was busy with a course in Basic Business Administration, with which he hoped to be able to land an office job. He had plans to show people how hard he could work and how loyal he could be. Hopefully within a few years he would be able to get a supervisor's job and start making decent money.

As he sat on the edge of the bed making notes and summarising he thought once again how fortunate he was to have had the opportunity to finish high school, something many of his peers had not been able to do.

One day he would be somebody. One day he would be respected and prosperous. Until then he would have to rely on his faith in God, the love of his family and his two-second smile.

Busted

"Arrogant idiot!" muttered James Huntingdon-Smythe to himself, "And an even bigger sycophantic idiot that published this garbage"

He threw the paper down on his mahogany desk in disgust.

"Just like the Vuvuzela to take our rejects and make a big song and dance out of it like it was their idea in the first place. Talk about blowing your own horn!"

He shoved the previous evening's Vuvuzela along with the other rival newspapers which he checked first thing every morning to one side of his desk and flicked the intercom button.

"Tracey, get Dirk in here now please."

"Right away sir."

While he waited he picked up the paper again and read the article with annoyance. He had just started the last paragraph when a knock at the door disturbed him,

"Come in."

Dirk took a deep breath and entered. His editor was known for his vacillating and sometimes stormy temper. A summons at short notice was enough to make any young journalist afraid of the reason.

"Sit!" barked James at him, "Look at this garbage!"

He tossed the paper in the general direction of Dirk, swivelled in his chair and sat glaring out of the window while Dirk read the front-page article and looked at the accompanying full-colour photograph.

"Return to Morality and Dignity", shouted the headline. Below and left of the headline was the photograph of Hugh Mitchell, impeccably dressed in an expensive and well-cut charcoal grey suit. He was addressing a crowd of young adults with an upright posture and raised index finger that made him look like a revivalist preacher.

"Hugh Mitchell, successful mining magnate and philanthropist, today launched the Add Values campaign. This project is aimed at young people and intended to encourage a return to old-fashioned values like dignity, hard work and moral purity..."

The article went on to describe at some length Hugh Mitchell's meteoric rise from young metallurgist to successful gold mining company chairman. This was followed by a fawning declaration that he was widely recognised and acknowledged for his moral integrity and dedicated work ethic.

"Young people all over the country would do well to follow the example of this great man and commit to celibacy, integrity and hard work for the good of themselves and the nation", concluded the article.

"Sanctimonious fool!" boomed James as Dirk finished the last line and looked up. "Considering he made his fortune in some rather shady deals and there have been rumours around town for years about his fairly liberal view of marital integrity, what a heap of tripe!"

Dirk ventured an opinion,

"It looks like he must have approached the Vuvuzela after you refused to put him on the front page."

"And they were no doubt only to happy to be the mouthpiece for the great Hugh Mitchell. A nice fuzzy piece on a Thursday night to make their readers feel good just before the weekend."

The following Monday morning James marched through the office, glaring at anyone who appeared not to be working. He rounded a corner and walked past the staff kitchen.

As he passed by something caught his eye and he turned back for a second look. Satisfied that his first impression had not misled him he strode into the kitchen and barked at Dirk Venter,

"Good grief man, what happened to you? Have you gone undercover to investigate a ring of hoboes?"

"No sir", Dirk looked at himself in the mirror-finish of the refrigerator and grimaced. He hadn't really noticed just how dishevelled he looked.

"Actually I spent most of the weekend in my car and haven't had a chance yet to go home for a shower and change of clothes."

"What earthly reason could you have for sleeping in your car? Your girlfriend give you the boot, landlord objected to your taste in music, well what?"

"Actually I didn't sleep much at all, I was on a stakeout outside a hotel."

James shook his head in dismay and annoyance,

"A stakeout! Since when did you cease to be a journalist and instead become the star of a bad cop movie?"

"I was being a journalist sir, the stakeout was in pursuit of a really good story."

"So go on then, tell me about this fantastic story that was worth spending the night in your car and arriving at the office looking like a walking charity sale."

"Can I bring it to your office in a short while sir? I'm just waiting for the lab. It will make more sense when you see the photos."

"Fine, but don't take all day. I don't have time to waste."

Dirk watched his boss storm out of the kitchen and returned to the tea and toast he had been preparing before being interrupted. Why did James Huntingdon-Smythe always have to enter and leave a room as if he were mounting a one-man military campaign? He ran the paper much like a front line regiment, with discipline and ruthlessness.

No wonder there were legends told about his days in the military before he turned to journalism. It seemed an odd choice of career after having been an intelligence officer. However the determination and efficiency with which he pursued stories, often involving corrupt politicians and similarly immoral individuals, soon earned him a reputation as an incredibly efficient investigative journalist if not a likeable one.

It had not been long before he was made a news editor and only a few years before he rose to his current position as editor in chief of one of Johannesburg's largest daily papers.

A little under an hour later, assorted colleagues watched with varied degrees of interest as Dirk headed for the editor's office armed with a brown envelope and a few pages of hastily scribbled notes.

James studied the contents of the envelope in some detail and then leant back with a satisfied smirk. His expression softened into what might not quite qualify as a smile, but was at least a close contender for the title,

"How did you get these?" he asked with curiosity. The photos he referred to lay face up and overlapping on the desk between him and Dirk.

"I have a friend in the hotel business. He found it strange that a businessman who lived in Joburg would book into a hotel in the same city on a Saturday night. When the businessman in question checked in and told the desk clerk that he was going up to his room and to give the room number to the lady who would ask for it later, my friend gave me a call."

"Looks like your friend has good instincts. Why would Hugh Mitchell book into a hotel 30 minutes from his home? Why would he arrive there in the early evening and leave instructions to give his room number to a lady later? A lady who arrives shortly after in her own car and then heads for the room without delay. Caught with his pants down in a manner of speaking."

"And then they stayed in the room the whole day Sunday, ordering room service meals and newspapers and only emerging to have a massage at the hotel gym. I decided to hang around and see what they got up to. They stayed Sunday night as well and left in the early hours of this morning before breakfast and before most of the staff and other guests were awake", said Dirk.

"Hmm, not a bad looking lady either", commented James. "Although quite what she sees in this idiot I'm not sure", he said, poking his finger into the recently developed image of Hugh Mitchell's face.

"Right, get your article written and proofed pronto. I want enough time to check it personally and still be able to get it into this afternoon's edition."

Dirk nodded and left hastily to do his boss's bidding.

"Tracey", James instructed via intercom, "Set up a meeting here with Hugh Mitchell early this afternoon. Tell him I will explain the reason only when he gets here, but that it is imperative that he attend."

"Well, what was so important that you had to drag

me here in the middle of the day. I'm a very busy man you know. I also had an early morning and am very tired so let's get to the point shall we."

"Actually Hugh", said James with a smirk, "It's due to your busyness the last two nights and the reason for your surreptitious early morning rising that we are here."

He reached into the cardboard folder that lay on the conference room table and produced a proof copy of Dirk's article, complete with an enlarged photo. From the weak light it was evident that the couple leaving via the hotel lobby were doing so very early in the morning.

" So, just how will you explain to your adoring fans what the leader of the Add Values campaign was doing leaving a hotel early in the morning with an attractive female companion?"

Hugh leant forward, placed his forearms on the table edge and stared at the article and photograph for a few moments before looking up,

"James, for your own good you'd better revise your front page and print some other story instead."

"Is that a threat?"

"No James, it's a suggestion. One that will save considerable embarrassment if it is accepted."

"Too late, it's already been sent to the printers."

"Then I suggest you put a hold on the printing, whip together a new front page and get it over to your printer immediately."

James looked at his watch and sneered with satisfaction,

"By now, the first batches will already have been printed and be in the trucks taking them to the distribution points."

"In that case you are correct, it's too late to avoid embarrassment. I assume this discussion is at an end then."

Hugh pushed back his chair, stood to his feet and turned to leave. Behind his back gloating smiles of victory were exchanged. The smiles vanished as he turned back into the room,

"Before I leave gentlemen, there is one thing I feel compelled to do."

He reached into his pocket, withdrew his wallet and opened it. The expectant faces of James and Dirk turned upwards to meet his gaze.

He rifled through the contents until he found what he was looking for. He flicked a small rectangle onto the table next to the proof. Editor and reporter both looked with horror at the small item he had produced, a wedding photo. Although obviously taken some years ago the smiling couple was distinctly recognisable.

Hugh leaned over the table, stabbed his finger at the front page photo and then at the smaller picture and said,

"That gentlemen, is my wife! Our house is being fumigated so we spent the weekend in a hotel. I dropped her at the airport early this morning to fly to the UK on business. Thankfully she will be out of the country for the next few days and won't have to view this drivel. I will of course make sure that a rival publication carries a prominent picture of my wife and I, all smiling and happy, in tomorrow's paper. Congratulations on making even bigger fools of yourselves than I could ever have hoped for."

Gangsters Paradise

Jeanette screamed.

"Hey, what do you think you're doing?!"

The brown eyes met hers for a brief mocking moment and then he was off, sprinting down the driveway with her handbag held in his left hand like a baton.

He ran between the electric sliding gate and the cement pillar, disturbing the safety beam. The gate stopped its slow progress, paused for a moment as if reflecting and then trundled back the way it had come. Her shocked stare down the road was interrupted by the sound of puffing and panting. She half-turned and saw the squat, kindly frame of Petros heading towards her with difficulty.

"*Hawu* madam, this *tsotsis* are everywhere nowadays."

"Did you see what happened?"

"Yes madam, he was hiding behind the bush outside. When you opened the gate and drove in he ran in behind the car. Then when you got out to open the garage he opened the passenger door and grabbed your handbag. I saw everything madam, but I couldn't get off the scaffolding fast enough to grab him, I'm sorry."

She smiled down at the man they had hired to build an extension to the house. He was a good, if unsophisticated man.

"Thanks Petros, I'm glad you tried to help. Now what? My cellphone is in my bag, and my purse, credit cards, everything!"

As she said the words rage overcame the shock. It was barely a month since their house was broken into while they were out with friends. It wasn't so much the loss of the TV and DVD player that bothered them, it was the violation of their home and sanctity.

Suddenly she remembered the monitored alarm system that Bill installed after the burglary. She felt cold metal pressing into her fingers and looked down at the keys clutched in her hand. Of course, the remote panic button. Maybe the security company could do something? She pressed the button and then re-considered. Who knew how long they would take to react?

"Petros, I'm going after him. He's not getting away with this!" She swung back into the driver's seat.

"Wait madam, we'll come with you. I'd like to grab that tsotsi and smack him good!"

He turned away, whistling and yelling towards the building site. The two nearest workers came running leaving only one man who was at the top of the scaffold. Petros and the two much younger men piled into Jeanette's car.

"Right madam lets go."

Jeanette already had the gate open and she charged the car down the driveway and into the street, pausing to decide which way to turn. Petros indicated left with his hand.

" Go this way madam. There's an open *veld* down this road. He'll probably go there, that's the way all the tsotsis go to get back to the township.

Jeanette took his suggestion and raced off down the road. They were almost to the end of the street when one of the men in the back seat shouted,

"There!"

He pointed at the veld where a lone figure could be

seen walking over the dusty surface towards the township just visible in the distance. The young man opened his window and hung out waving his fist and yelling wildly.

Jeanette could not understand a word of his rapid isiZulu but assumed it was not polite. Petros and the third man did likewise, opening their windows and shouting threats at the distant figure.

Jeanette sped up to overtake a *bakkie* and try catch up to the thief. Piet Van Staden, a local

plumber who was driving the bakkie, glanced at the car that had overtaken him. Suddenly he jammed the accelerator to the floor. There was a furious clatter from the diesel motor followed by a shrill whine as the turbo kicked in. Seeing a young attractive white woman driving at speed down the road towards the local township accompanied by three yelling and gesticulating black men his reading of the situation was as swift as it was incorrect. He assumed that she was the victim of a hijacking and was being taken to the township under duress to be raped or killed or both. Ever the knight in shining overalls he gave chase to effect a rescue.

At the same time as Piet was coming to Jeanette's rescue a response vehicle from the security company pulled into her driveway in answer to the silent distress signal. The builder who had remained behind briefly explained to the reaction officer what had happened and showed him in which direction Jeanette's car had gone. The reaction officer headed in the same direction to see if he could assist.

" Idiot", spat Jeanette as Piet Van Staden's bakkie came roaring up behind her, lights flashing and hooter blaring. She slowed down to check in which direction the thief was headed and to see if there was a way to intercept him.

"Over there madam", said Petros, "There's a dirt road just past the traffic light. The taxis use it to avoid the traffic and get into the township."

As she sped up the security vehicle was approaching from behind. The officer spotted her car being closely followed by a bakkie. Fearing that it contained accomplices of the thief he gunned his motor, unholstered his pistol and used his two-way radio to call for backup.

Jeanette slowed down at the traffic light that stared redly at her, but decided not to stop. She glanced in all directions to make sure the coast was clear then accelerated through the intersection. She did not want to lose her quarry over a traffic signal.

Piet Van Staden, who was still right behind and attempting to get her to pull over, followed suit. The reaction officer who was only a few metres behind Piet became the third vehicle to run the red light. Piet's hooting woke a metro police officer who had parked his patrol car in the bushes at the side of the road and was spending a peaceful afternoon dreaming about fighting crime.

He opened his eyes to see the odd procession storm though the red light slow down and slide off into a cloud of dust as they attacked the dirt road. He was fully awake in an instant flicked switches to get the blue lights flashing and siren wailing then tore off in pursuit.

The thief who was now casually strolling along examining the contents of Jeanette's handbag heard the commotion and glanced over his shoulder. His eyes widened in disbelief as he spotted the odd collection of pursuers.

He threw the bag away from him as he ran like a lizard shedding its tail hoping it would distract them, then headed for a piece of stony ground where he knew the cars would have difficulty following him. This ploy bought him some time but was not an ideal solution. He would still have to leave the area sooner or later and cross at least one road to reach the township. That would expose him to being chased yet again. For the time being he disappeared into a clump of thorn trees.

The vehicles skidded to a dusty stop and all of the occupants leapt out. Piet had been so busy attempting to rescue Jeanette that he did not notice the fleeing thief. He now came running wielding a piece of lead pipe like a sword, St George out to slay the three dragons or at least give them all a good beating.

The reaction officer made the assumption that Piet was in cahoots with the thief and was trying to prevent any pursuit of his accomplice. He drew himself up to his full height and shouted,

"Stop!"

As his full height was 5'2" and his voice resembled a squeaky toy clogged with lint nobody stopped, or even noticed. He cleared his throat and tried again,

"Stop or I'll shoot!"

This time he was noticed. Piet turned and surveyed him with distaste and amusement. He was dressed from head to toe completely in black resembling a Ninja from the east, or at least the *East Rand*. The resemblance stopped at the outfit though. He was chubby and pasty faced, with a weak attempt at a macho moustache clinging hopefully to his upper lip. He looked like a schoolboy going to a costume party.

He did however have a gun, so everybody stopped and looked at him. Now that he was the centre of attention he was not sure what to do. The situation was further complicated when he heard a voice behind him,

" Put the gun down you stupid *lightie*. Just now someone gets hurt."

In his eagerness to be the local Rambo he had forgotten about the metro police officer. He turned slightly and saw a menacing figure in blue and khaki pointing a police-issue pistol at him. He hesitated, unsure of what to do.

"Listen idiot, I am a police officer. Now do it!"

He complied and slowly bent down to place the gun on the ground.

The police officer kept the pistol aimed in the general direction of the others and removed his sunglasses with his left hand. After carefully hanging them from his shirt pocket he regarded the group with a piercing if slightly bleary stare,

"Right, just what is going on here?"

A flurry of sound came back to him.

"Hold on, hold on, one at a time. Let's start with the lady" He produced a notebook and pencil from his shirt pocket. "Firstly, what's your name? Then tell me briefly what happened to cause you to drive through a red traffic light and end up here."

"My name is Jeanette, Jeanette Cooper. I had just arrived at home when someone stole my handbag out of my car. I chased after him and ended up here."

"And is one of these three the suspect?" said the policeman looking at the builders who were doing their best to fade into the background.

"Oh no, these three gentlemen were kind enough to come with and help me. They are doing some building work for me"

"So where is the thief now?"

"He's hiding among those trees", was the thin comment from the security officer.

"Well make yourself useful and go see if you can grab him and bring him here."

"My backup is already busy with that." He pointed his finger to illustrate.

In the commotion and questioning nobody noticed another security vehicle pull up on the other side of the veld. An officer climbed out of this vehicle and released a large dog from a cage in the back.

" Go help your colleague while I ask some more questions. If you catch the call me."

While the two security officers and the dog set about flushing the criminal from the bushes the policeman turned his attention to Piet Van Staden. So far his presence was a mystery, but one easily solved by means of a few direct questions.

The investigation was soon over, notes scribbled and pencil and pad safely pocketed. Now the policeman unhooked his sunglasses and put them on with a flourish.

"You lot wait here in case I need you."

He started heading towards the scraggly nest of thorn trees. The two security officers were approaching the task of apprehending the criminal with a lot of enthusiasm but very little finesse. They blundered about falling over fallen branches and swearing, giving a fair impression of marula-drunk elephants.

The dog stood to one side carefully sniffing around and looking intelligently into the bushes. Clearly he was the superior life form in the immediate vicinity. As the security herd smashed and stumbled deeper into the trees the criminal hiding within took fright and bolted.

The dog gave chase, barking and snarling. The criminal, hearing the fearsome sound behind, decided he was in danger of becoming lunch for the dog. He put on a burst of speed, but this food was not nearly fast enough and the dog caught him within a few metres. Teeth clamped to the cuff of his trouser leg and he went down in a heap of dust and panic. His arms covered his face and he screamed. The well-trained dog released the mouthful of cloth and simply stood over him growling a warning not to move.

The policeman who had been approaching with something closely resembling a run now huffed, puffed and blew to a halt with pistol drawn and handcuffs at the ready. He took several immense breaths and croaked,

"You're under arrest." He cuffed the suspect and started prodding him towards the patrol car.

"Meet me at the station, I'll need statements from both of you", he called back to the security officers.

He reached his car, safely stowed the suspect in the back and ordered the remaining participants in the drama to follow him to the police station so he could take their statements as well.

Jeanette glared at the suspect cowering behind a car window.

"Will there be a charge so you can take him away and lock him up", she asked.

"No charge ma'am, we'll lock him up for you for free." He laughed at his own corniness.

"Don't worry. We'll throw the book at him, or at least hit him a few times with it." He laughed again, alone as before.

He fished in his pocket for his car keys, hooked them and was getting ready to leave for the station when a tremendous yelling of threats and profanities filtered across the open veld.

The security officers had leashed the dog and returned to the bakkie. They found only skid marks and a few drops of oil in the road instead. The dog handler had been so eager to show off his skills that he had left his bakkie unlocked and the keys in the

ignition. In street language this constituted a neatly
printed and embossed invitation to any other
criminals who were in the area. Two criminals were
indeed nearby and they were pleased to RSVP and
steal the vehicle.

The officers shouted and stared down the road but
there was now no sign of the bakkie anywhere. It was
their yelling opinions of the car thieves and their
mothers down the road that had attracted the
policeman's attention.

Not impressed he sighed and removed his
sunglasses. More work. He locked his patrol car,
checked that the suspect was securely handcuffed to
the door handle and turned away kicking an innocent
stone in frustration. The stone curved neatly upwards
and struck the back of Piet Van Staden's bakkie. It
clanged off the metal number plate, leaving a small
dent between the letters G and P. Gauteng Province or
as it was affectionately known locally: Gangsters
Paradise.

The policeman drew his notebook and pencil
again, sighed and headed across the veld towards the
two furious men and one smiling dog.

The Weekend

"Hey Sally, where are last month's sales stats?"

"Probably on your desk Al, I gave them to you last week."

"Oh."

From the office next door came the sound of papers being shuffled.

"Got it", called Al triumphantly.

He came through the doorway. "Won't you find out from Bill's secretary what time he is going out for lunch?"

"OK." Sally made the call and then went to give the information to her boss.

"Good I'll go up and sneak the report into his in-tray while he's out."

Sally returned to her desk and wondered how someone so careless and incompetent had made it as far as Sales Manager. Perhaps the office grapevine was correct and he had only been promoted because he was married to the younger sister of one of the directors. There was speculation that he had only married her to advance his career.

The total lack of respect and caring with which he spoke to his wife seemed to support this gossip, Sally had been appalled on the few occasions she had overheard him on the telephone with her. How any woman could stay married to that pig she didn't know.

In addition to his incompetence, for which she often had to cover up, he was always hitting on her. Talk in the ladies bathroom indicated that she was not alone. Al seemed to have quite a reputation for flirting around the office. One day he would come unstuck.

Later that week she was making coffee when she bumped into Bill Jenkins, the Sales and Marketing Director.

"Morning Mr Jenkins", she said brightly.

"Hello Sally, how are you?"

"Fine thanks Mr Jenkins."

"You don't look fine. You look frustrated. Come on tell me the truth, off the record", he said smiling.

"Well, I guess I'm just a little bored. I've been Assistant Sales Manager for three years and..."

"And that idiot Al keeps taking the credit for your hard work."

"That's not what I was going to say", she said blushing.

"No, it's what you were thinking though isn't it Do you think I haven't noticed? Every single month I have to remind him to hand in his sales report. And every month it mysteriously appears a few days later in the middle of my in-tray. Does he think I'm that stupid?"

Sally hid a smile. So she was not the only one who noticed Al's incompetence.

Jenkins continued,

"Just hang in there Sally, Al won't be in that job forever you know. In fact if he wasn't married to George Taylor's sister, I doubt he would have lasted this long."

After Jenkins had left for his office, Sally stood a few minutes in the canteen to digest the conversation. Al had made at least one enemy on the board, could there be others? She would bide her time and be civil, if not actually friendly, to him and wait for his inevitable demise. Or maybe even help prompt it.

Three weeks passed until one day Al made his next subtle pass at her. They were both preparing to leave the office one afternoon when Al looked out of the window and said,

"Man, look at that sunshine. I wouldn't mind going down to the coast for a weekend break. I have some air miles to spare, but Janet's such a stick-in-the-mud when it comes to going away."

Boldly she said, "OK Al, I'll go with you."

"What!"

"Oh come on Al. We both know that's what you want. You've hinted about spending a weekend together since we met."

"Yes, but I never thought you'd agree to go."

"Look I'd also like to get away from Joburg for a couple of days. Besides, it might be fun." She winked and said, "Bye, see you tomorrow."

Halfway through the next morning Al appeared at Sally's desk with a grin and a brochure.

"Hey Salls, how about this weekend, can you make it?"

"I don't think I have plans."

"Good, I was thinking of the Wild Coast. We can leave on Friday after work and fly back on Sunday afternoon."

"What about your wife?"

"I already told her that I need to go down to Durban for a new store opening on Saturday and Sunday."

They arranged that both of them would come to work on the Friday with their bags already packed. They would leave the office 30 minutes apart and meet later at the airport to "avoid suspicion" as Sally had put it. She had no desire to be the latest topic of discussion on the office grapevine.

Al agreed. Although he seemed to have no qualms about cheating on his wife, he was concerned that he might sabotage his career if the directors found out that he, a married man, was taking his deputy away for the weekend while leading his wife to believe that he was on company business. George Taylor in particular would probably have not only a professional interest, but would surely seek revenge on the man who was unfaithful to his sister.

The next morning Sally had been at work only a short time when she discovered a small box of Belgian chocolates in the top drawer of her desk. Taped to the lid was a small card in an envelope. The note inside read:

Hi Sexy, Looking forward to our weekend together.
Let's put the wild back into the Wild Coast!
Don't forget, Friday at 18H30 in domestic departures.

Love, Al

Sally giggled. Al may not be everyone's favourite, but there was a kind of bumbling charm to this gesture. Maybe if he were this attentive to his wife he would have a happier life.

Early on Friday morning Al called Sally to his office and asked her to do him a favour as he had a full schedule.

"Won't you arrange to have some flowers sent to Janet at our place this afternoon? She should be home around half past four. Have them put a card in with a message, I'll miss you over the weekend Love Al. Something like that. Should make her happy for a while and stop her from being suspicious."

"Sure. In fact I need to go out just now, I'll do it at the same time. I'll write the card myself and arrange the delivery for about five. Is that OK?"

"Perfect. Here let me give you my address."

Sally walked away smiling. Al had just helped her solve one small problem without realising it.

At ten past five Sally left the office. She would be at the airport well before she was due to meet Al. Not that she minded, it would give her a chance to sit somewhere and think about what was about to happen..

Al left his office at four thirty and headed upstairs to the staff canteen. His Friday *drink with the boys* was a regular event. Today he did not really feel like going but had decided to not go would make people wonder where he was. Having people interested in his whereabouts was not wise on this particular day.

At twenty past six Sally was seated in a coffee shop overlooking the domestic departures hall at Johannesburg International Airport. Through the leaves of a plastic plant she saw Al arrive and stand near the check in counters, fidgeting. He cast several nervous glances towards the entrance. Anyone watching him would have accurately assumed that he was waiting to meet someone.

Sally was the only person in the airport who knew who he was about to meet. Within a few minutes she caught sight of Janet entering the hall and striding towards Al with anger and purpose, a small card in her hand. She had taken the bait. It had been relatively simple for Sally to "mix up" the card that the florist had handed her with the one which Al had given her with the chocolates.

"Bill please", she said.

Kidnapped

"…and what was the reaction from our saviour and king brothers and sisters. Did he condemn? Did he accuse? Did he rage? No, he silently reached down towards the ground. Many watching may have assumed he was feeling for a stone with which to begin the punishment. Instead brothers and sisters, he pointed his forefinger and wrote, yes wrote in the sand. What he wrote we will never know in this life, maybe never in eternity. Then he told the Pharisees that the law did indeed decree that the woman caught in adultery should be stoned to death, but that the one amongst them who had no sin in his own life would have to throw the first stone. This surprised them, shocked them, angered them, but they said nothing and quietly left. Maybe they grumbled amongst themselves, but still they left. The woman was as shocked as they and may have wondered if Jesus was planning to enforce judgement on her all on his own. Instead of judgement he gave her forgiveness, but also a stern warning to sin no more. The truth we learn here is this, the law is the law, but grace can overcome the law."

During this last sentence *Dominee* Douw Pieterse came out from behind the pulpit which he had a paragraph ago thumped with the palm of his hand to emphasise the tension of the scene described. Behind the pulpit he represented the law, but out in the open with his hands spread wide and a benevolent smile on his face he represented grace.

Slightly theatrical it might be but the congregation seemed to relax and enjoy the moment. Seated in the front row Mrs. Sanette (Sannie to her friends) Pieterse could only see the senior elders to right and left of her, but even here there were some relieved smiles. This type of preaching was one of the things that so endeared her husband to his congregation.

She had been in this church for a long time and knew that many in the pews behind and even a few up front had reason enough to hope that grace did indeed triumph over the judgement of the law. She herself had some reason, even though her wild child teenage and early adult days were 30 years behind her and either long forgotten or at least never spoken of by those in the congregation who had known her since her youth.

After the service Douw and Sannie circulated around the church hall greeting congregation members, many of whom were juggling cups of tea or coffee, slices of cake and children.

The ministerial couple were widely loved and respected in the community, if slightly pitied due to their inability to have children. Their assertion that they were happy and that the church was all the family they needed was generally believed and accepted. Most who knew them thought of them as a happy and near perfect couple.

The few who knew them well and long enough to pick up on the frequent but hastily concealed looks of annoyance and tense atmosphere also knew enough to stay out of it. Mostly they had enough demons of their own to wrestle with and did not need to jump into the ring with the personal issues of Dominee and Mrs. Pieterse.

Douw was known to them as a loving pastor, a good friend but a formidable and unflinching enemy. Like several others in his denomination he had entered the ministry to seek absolution from his past and would not welcome interference, especially from those who had known him since his pre-seminary days.

They had joined their current church when Douw was appointed as junior minister to assist the ageing man who had been at the helm for more years than most could remember. On the older man's retirement Douw had been asked to take over the role of senior minister. That had been some 15 years ago and he had run the church with wise efficiency. Membership and income from offerings had increased and he had earned the approval of the denomination's central synod and the respect of the congregation.

Ostensibly, they had a good and successful life. That all changed one Friday night.

Sannie had spent the evening watching TV before deciding to go to bed at about half past ten. She had become accustomed to many evenings alone while her husband attended to church business or "counselled" errant members, the identities and sinful details of whom he could naturally not divulge even to her.

Tonight was a little unusual as he generally called her by ten to tell her he was on his way or to say he would be later still. If she had suspicions about the whereabouts of and participants in these lengthy "counselling" sessions she kept them to herself.

The one time Douw had accidentally dialled her number from the speed dial on his cellphone causing her to hear background noises more in keeping with a brothel than a church office had been glossed over and never really discussed. But it had hovered in the air over the marriage since that night and haunted their relationship, specifically demonising their intimacy that was infrequent and never initiated by Sannie.

She was well provided for, had a nice house and

car and was respected as the minister's wife. She had long ago decided that if not prying too much was the asking price for her lifestyle, she would pay up with a smile.

She decided to go to bed instead of sitting up waiting for him to call, perhaps he had just forgotten to call, or to charge his cellphone battery. She read for a few minutes in bed and then drifted off to sleep.

Finally at a quarter to midnight the phone rang. A quick glimpse at the screen confirmed the call came from Douw's phone.

"Where are you, why didn't you call earlier?"

I've been kidnapped."

This short sentence jolted her out of her sleepiness and into an upright position.

"What!"

"I'm OK, so far. One of them wants to talk to you"

A gruff voice came on the line,

"Mrs Pieterse, we have your husband. If you want him back unharmed, you'd better co-operate with us. Further instructions will follow tomorrow. In the meantime do not go to the police or tell anyone else. If you do we will know and it could be dangerous for Douw."

The call was abruptly terminated. She couldn't help thinking the voice sounded a little familiar. Probably she had just watched too many movie kidnappings and was subconsciously associating the voice with all the villains she had seen over the years.

Sannie fell back against the pillows and stared blindly at the cellphone. She felt unable to move or even think. Besides, where would she go? What would she do? The man had been very clear about not involving the police or even telling anyone else.

She spent the rest of the night sleeping in short snatches, waking every few minutes to check the screen of her cellphone just in case she had missed a call, unlikely as she had both the landline telephone and cellphone on the bed just centimetres from her face. Besides, they had told her they would only phone again in the morning.

She got out of bed as the sun was beginning to backlight the bedroom curtains. With a cup of coffee in one hand and cellphone in the other she sat in the quiet lounge and tried to decide what to do. She hated just sitting and waiting like this. In a way it was a blessing that they had never been able to have children, at least she would not have to explain to them where their dad had disappeared to. On the other hand it meant she was all alone in this.

After a while she stood up. She couldn't do this. She had to tell someone, have someone to talk to while she waited. A name dropped into her consciousness; Flip Steyn. He was an old friend and her one-time boyfriend, although Douw knew little of this. He knew Flip mostly as an old friend of Sannie's and a long serving elder in the church. He knew nothing of the teenage pregnancy and subsequent hushed up and illegal abortion that was the probable cause of Sannie's infertility. Flip had been a policeman for most of his adult life, eventually taking early retirement after a distinguished career as a top class detective.

Within an hour Flip was in the lounge listening thoughtfully to her story and drinking his usual black coffee. While she spoke he scribbled in a small notebook.

After she finished speaking he sat in silence for a few minutes re-reading his notes and making additions in between the original sentences. Eventually he looked up,

"Sannie, you sure you don't want to go to the

police with this?"

She shook her head, unable to speak. Flip saw tears forming in her eyes.

"In that case, of course I'll do what I can to help. But you must remember I'm retired from the police service so I don't have access to the resources and manpower they would have."

"I'm not sure I could trust them, I trust you"

Flip looked at the tear-stained cheeks and watery eyes before him and smiled gently,

"I'll do my best for you Sannie, you know that."

"Thank you."

"Have they contacted you since last night?"

"No, they said they'd call me today. They told me not to go to the police or tell anyone. Do you think they know you're here and that's why they haven't contacted me?"

"I doubt it, besides if they really want money they'll contact you anyway. If you don't mind there are a few things I need to double check"

"Sure"

"You said you were relieved when the phone rang because you were starting to worry about Douw. How did you know it was him?"

"The call was from his cellphone"

"Strange, I would have thought they would be afraid of his phone being tracked and used to find them. Actually it would be kind of handy if we were able to track his phone, I don't suppose Douw subscribes to a cell tracing service? You know the kind of thing that allows family members to see where you are in case of an emergency etc."

"Not likely", she muttered half to herself.

In response to the question in Flip's eyes she tilted her head and studied the burgundy carpet.

"Come on Sannie, out with it. If I'm going to help you I need to know anything unusual that was going on in Douw's life. It may be relevant."

"Nothing unusual, just that I get the feeling Douw would rather I not know where he is most of the time. Can we leave it at that?"

"OK, for now. The other thing is, you said the man said that if you went to the police it could be dangerous for Douw. Were those his exact words, I mean did he call him Douw?"

"Yes he did."

"That's a little unusual. In my experience kidnappers seldom use victim's names. They will say things like your child, your husband etc. It helps them to stay emotionally detached."

"So what can we do now?"

"Nothing more we can do now but wait."

"You want some more coffee Flip?"

"Yes please."

Sannie had been gone less than five minutes when the sound of a ringing cellphone overshadowed the clinking of cups and saucers from the kitchen. She ran wide-eyed into the lounge

"Do you think it's them?"

"Might be", said Flip glancing at the phone's display. The call was from an unidentified number. Very easy to hide the number on a cellphone he thought.

"Answer it."

With white knuckles and shallow breath Sannie answered the phone. Flip handed the notebook and pencil to Sannie, knowing she would probably receive instructions from the kidnappers. He heard only one side of the conversation.

"Yes, yes, I understand. Don't worry I will co-operate. Hold on let me get that down."

She scribbled an address as she listened.

"Yes I know where it is, I'll bring it myself. Now please can I talk to my husband?"

While she waited to see if her request would be honoured, Flip picked up his own phone and dialled Douw's cellphone number on a hunch. It was engaged.

"Douw, are you OK? Don't worry I'll get the money. How did it happen? But how…yes I suppose it is very dark outside the church office. Douw, Douw…"

She put down the phone.

"They hung up on me". She sank back speechless against the cushions, drained after this short conversation. Flip reached out gently and removed the notebook from her clenched fingers. It contained the name of a local shopping centre and a number. Sannie recovered slightly and looked at him,

"I'm supposed to take R25,000 to that shopping centre at 12," she said motioning to the paper in Flip's hand.

"Can you raise that kind of money?"

"Yes we have around R30,000 in a savings account. It was supposed to be for an overseas cruise for us next year. Now we won't be able to go."

Another question welled up in Flip's eyes but this time Sannie didn't notice. He thought it a strange comment for a woman whose husband had been kidnapped. He had been aware of tension in the marriage for some time but had not realised just how deep the cracks had spread. She seemed genuinely upset about Douw's kidnapping one minute and then disaffected the next. Now she bustled away into the kitchen to finish making coffee.

Flip dialled Douw's cellphone number again on

the same hunch. "The subscriber you have dialled is not available at present, please try again later." Douw's phone was definitely switched on during the call to Sannie and now it was off. He was certain the call had been made from Douw's cellphone. The smell of fish hung over this whole situation.

When Sannie returned with the coffee they started planning. She was adamant that she did not want the police involved, even when Flip pointed out that the police could get an urgent court order for a location trace by the cellphone network. They would be able to approximate the location from which any recent calls using Douw's phone had been made. She just wanted to pay the money and bring the whole incident to a close. She did however ask,

"Can't we file a missing persons report with the police, just in case they spot his car or something?"

"They will only open a missing person's case after 48 hours, and are likely to ask some awkward questions about the circumstances of Douw's disappearance. Either we tell them the whole kidnapping story or we leave them out of this", was his advice to her.

"I'd better start making arrangements to get the money out of our account if I'm to make it to the shopping centre on time."

"Will the bank release that kind of cash to you?"

"I'm sure they will if I go in personally. Can you come with me? I'll tell them you are a friend and ex-policeman so they don't worry too much about a woman walking around alone with a lot of cash."

"Of course I can. I'll get one of my guys to follow us for safety, in an unmarked car."

Sannie had temporarily forgotten that Flip now ran a private security firm, specialising in the surveillance and escorting of high value goods and cash.

"That's probably a good idea, as long as he stays out of sight, in case I'm being watched. They were very insistent about me not telling anybody."

"Don't worry, I'll make sure he keeps a low profile. It'll only take a quick call to arrange it. He can bring one of our special briefcases back with him, the type we use for transporting cash. They have a miniature tracking device built in. Bit of a weak signal but it works at close range. Might help to track down the kidnappers once we've got Douw back."

"It won't help, the man said I must put it in an A4 envelope and stick it in the post office box with the number he gave me, it will be unlocked."

Sannie's memory was suddenly jogged by one of Flip's earlier comments.

"Sorry Flip, I forgot till now. Douw had a satellite-tracking device fitted to his car a few weeks ago after there were some cars stolen in the neighbourhood. Do you think it could be used to track him down?"

"Maybe. If it hasn't been disarmed and if he's near the car. But it would take a court order or at least a formal request from the police to get the company to activate it, unless..."

"Unless...?" echoed Sannie.

"Unless you could convince them the car was stolen and not mention Douw's disappearance at all. They might activate the signal just to get a location so they can send out a reaction crew. If you mention hijacking or kidnapping or anything like that they'll call the police immediately. But if they think it's just a regular theft they'll probably just send out one of their own teams."

Seeing the look of hopeful expectancy on her face he asked,

"Do you think you can do it?"

"If you help me. I'll do my best"

"There must be some kind of document from the tracking company with activation codes etc. They'll probably ask you for information from it before doing anything. Any idea where it is?"

"If Douw has such a document it'll be in his files. He's very pedantic about filing everything. Hold on. I'll go look in his study."

While he waited Flip finished his coffee and stared through the glass door onto the shadowy patio and the pool that was beginning to shimmer in response to the rising sun.

He had just carried his empty cup through to the kitchen when Sannie reappeared, carrying a document with subdued triumph.

"I think this is it", she said.

Flip examined the piece of paper and confirmed that it was the correct document.

"Let's make the call now, give them as much time as possible to locate the car. But first we need to get your story right."

She nodded and Flip began explaining to her how to handle the call and what to say to the operator at the tracking company. He also wrote down on a separate piece of paper all the information he believed would be required to establish Sannie's identity as well as the legitimacy of the situation.

He listened while she made the call. She managed to sound suitably distressed but still totally coherent and able to communicate the required information.

She explained to the operator that she had swapped cars with her husband for the day as he was taking hers in for service and had looked outside to find his car missing from the yard. She also left her cellphone number with the operator, mentioning that her husband was a church minister who was busy counselling that day and would have his own phone off most of the time.

Flip told Sannie to go and fetch whatever documentation she needed to get the money released from the bank. While she was upstairs he made a call to his office, arranging for a specialist reaction officer in plain clothes and an unmarked car to come to the street where Sannie lived but to park on the corner several houses away and wait there.

If the house was being watched the arrival of a lone family friend who was also a church elder would not necessarily arouse suspicion, but a second vehicle and person probably would. Besides he needed the officer within reach but not too close. It was easier to observe any suspicious activity near the house from a slight distance.

Calling up the stairs that he was going for a short walk around the neighbourhood, he left the house via the door that led from the kitchen to the back yard. The lawn was soft and dewy under his leather loafers and damp pieces of recently cut grass clung to the polished surfaces. He came around past the swimming pool and down the narrow corridor between the garage and boundary wall, stopping almost level with the front of the garage. He hung back slightly, half-hidden in the long shadow created by the rising sun and the west-facing wall of the garage.

A few minutes spent watching and listening revealed nothing more sinister in the neighbourhood than a cat across the road studying some local birds with a look that spoke of breakfast. He left his hiding place and headed casually down the street, hands in pockets and seemingly carefree.

Eight front lawns passed him by until he came to the street corner where the security officer sat reading a newspaper as if waiting for someone. A quick glance through the windscreen confirmed that the occupant was indeed glancing over the edge of the paper and watching the street as he was trained to do.

Most of Flip's people were ex police detectives with good experience. On top of this he trained and re-trained them until they met his own personal standard. He walked a few metres past the car then swung and faced back the other way. No sign of a careless observer caught off guard. As he approached the driver's side the window wound down.

"Anything?"

"No sir, not that I can see."

Flip opened his mouth to speak again then tensed, hearing a vehicle approach. A second of careful listening assured him it was only a municipal waste disposal truck performing a garbage collection down the street.

"I'll be leaving with Mrs Pieterse shortly. Follow us and make sure you are the only one doing so." The officer nodded his assent and returned to his newspaper.

Flip started back towards the Pieterse's house and was passed by a dustman who leapt from the back of the slowly moving truck and ran up one of the driveways, whistling and yelling to his colleague who was likewise engaged on the other side of the road.

The garbage worker attempted to set a new land speed record down the driveway with the wheels on the bin rumbling furiously in protest, Flip took advantage of the distraction. He stepped into the street and walked level with the still creeping truck for a few metres to confuse any secret observer. As it drew level with the doorway in which Sannie now stood he slipped back around the truck and up the pathway.

"Ready to go?"

"Yes Flip, I think I've got everything."

"Right, we'll go in my car. My guy will follow us

at a distance."

"What guy? I don't see anyone."

"That's the whole idea. Let's go."

Flip nosed his car out into the road and drove towards the stop street on the corner. He indicated right and the security officer pulled off in the opposite direction, passing him with no sign of recognition. He drove slowly down towards the main road, knowing that the officer would by now have finished doing a quick drive-by check of the area around the Pieterse's house and be coming around the block to intercept his route.

As he waited at the traffic light Flip glanced in the rear-view mirror and smiled slightly as he observed the other vehicle coming out of a side street a hundred metres behind. The officer hung well back so as not to make it obvious that they were together. This tactic would also put anyone deciding to follow Flip between the two vehicles and thus easy to control.

The mini-convoy reached the shopping centre without incident, the officer still following at a distance. Flip and Sannie had decided to make use of the bank in the centre rather than her usual branch for two reasons. Firstly it meant minimal distance to transport the cash as the post office specified by the kidnappers was in the same centre. Secondly she was well known to the staff at her usual branch and did not want to cause gossip by being seen to draw a large amount of cash.

It was fairly easy to convince a helpful banker that her credentials were in order and get him to arrange for the R25,000 to be drawn from the safe. Her story that they were having an extension built onto their house and needed to pay the builder a deposit in cash was readily accepted. While they waited for the money to be brought to the banker's office he asked

her if she would like the bank to arrange a security
guard to accompany her. She nodded towards Flip,
whom she had earlier introduced as a family friend
and said,

"Mr Steyn here is in the security business himself.
I'm sure he's all the protection I need."

Flip reached down next to his chair and placed the
high-security briefcase, which he had earlier collected
from the security officer's car, on the banker's desk.
The young man nodded in understanding. Within
minutes the cash arrived and the banker checked and
supervised the packing of the money into the
briefcase. After Sannie had signed the receipt he
stood, shook hands with both her and Flip and wished
them well.

They left the bank and walked to a stationery shop
a few doors down. Here Sannie purchased a set of
large padded envelopes. It was still just under an hour
until they were due to place the cash in the post office
box so they returned to Flip's car, parked it around a
corner well out of sight of the post office just in case.

Flip packed the money into the envelopes, locked
them into the briefcase and placed it carefully in the
boot of his car. He then looked up and nodded slightly
to the security officer who was parked across the
street. The younger man gave only the briefest nod in
return before returning once again to his newspaper,
doing a fine job of appearing to be a bored husband
waiting for his wife to finish shopping.

Flip and Sannie returned to the row of businesses
and entered a small coffee shop to kill time until the
cash drop was due.

At ten minutes to twelve Sannie left the coffee
shop and went to Flip's car, alone in case she was
being watched. He stayed in the coffee shop that
conveniently looked across at the post office. He

watched Sannie walk into the passage that housed the post office boxes.

While he waited for her to come back out he glanced around to see if he could see anyone suspicious, working on the assumption that they would stay near the hand over point. He was pleased to see his employee doing likewise while pretending to study some puppies through the transparent façade of a pet shop.

He hoped the kidnappers would not realise that the area was being watched. His gut feel told him they were amateurs and likely to make some elementary mistakes that would allow him to spot the person collecting the cash.

Sannie was barely out of the passage when he had his suspect. The man approached from the parking lot glancing around and carrying an empty shopping bag in one hand. Flip quickly reached into his jacket pocket for the small but powerful digital camera.

He only managed to take two shots before his suspect disappeared into the passage. He looked in the direction of the security officer to signal him to keep close and noticed with pride that the officer's attention had shifted from the puppies to the passage entrance.

He had obviously come to the same conclusion as Flip and was ready to follow the suspect as soon as he came out. This youngster was sharp and Flip made a mental note to keep a closer eye on him, he could well have a bright future if this was his usual standard of work.

Within a few minutes the man returned, his shopping bag now showing signs of being almost full. This time Flip was able to take seven photos at different angles as the suspect walked between the shoppers and disappeared into the parking lot.

As the man passed the pet shop the security officer started angling through the parking lot, giving the appearance of walking in an aimless zigzag but actually following at a discreet distance.

Flip still had the camera in his hand when Sannie arrived, breathless and twittering,

"Do you think they'll come for the money soon?" she said slipping into the fake-leather booth.

"They already have. You were hardly out of the passage when the money was collected."

"Well, shouldn't we do something about it?"

"Don't worry, he's being followed"

"So, what do we do now?"

"We wait", he replied. "They have the money and they should contact you shortly. I don't think they will risk us going to the police at this stage by messing around. We might as well go back to your place and wait there."

He stood to leave and then sat down again.

"Before we go, I don't suppose you know this man?" he asked indicating a face on the camera's LCD screen.

"Yes", she said with surprise. "That's Willem Bezuidenhout, one of Douw's old buddies. He hasn't seen him in years. Good thing too, he's a real rubbish!"

"I have a feeling Douw has indeed seen him, he's the one who collected the money."

"Told you he was trouble, one of Douw's old friends and now he's involved in his kidnapping."

"Not quite sure how he fits in yet, maybe we'll find out later."

"Actually Flip, I think it may have been him on the phone. At the time I thought the voice sounded familiar then decided it was nothing. I think I may have recognised his voice after all these years."

"Interesting. If we don't hear from them soon regarding Douw's safe release we'll know where to start looking."

Flip paused as he noticed Sannie's worried look,

"Don't worry, I'm sure they'll be in contact soon to let you know about Douw. They want money not trouble. Let's have another coffee and then we'll go back to your place and wait to hear from them."

Flip was halfway through his black java and toying with the empty sugar packet when his cellphone rang. It was his security officer calling to give an update on Willem Bezuidenhout's movements since leaving the post office. He headed straight for a bank branch where the officer observed him making a substantial cash deposit at one of the tellers. After this he left the centre and drove to a house in the suburbs, presumably his own. He was currently still in the house with the officer watching from a safe distance.

After thanking the young man and commenting on his good work Flip leant back against the padded bench to absorb this information.

They were not quite as amateurish as he had first thought. The pick-up had been clumsy but using a bank account deposit was clever. Now the money could either be withdrawn in a lump sum from any branch of the same bank anywhere in the country, or in smaller amounts from any ATM. Also it would be different notes so even marked ban

k notes would have been of little help. Of course the transaction and account could be traced via the banks records, but that would require time and a court order.

The kidnappers were obviously relying on Sannie not going to the police until Douw was safely returned, if at all. Even if she did go the authorities later Flip was sure that the money would be withdrawn quickly and then the account never used again. It was possible the account didn't even belong to one of the kidnappers or had been specially opened for this purpose under a false name.

A short while later Flip and Sannie were back at her house drinking yet more coffee when her cellphone rang again. It was the satellite tracking company. The operator explained that they had tracked the vehicle to the parking lot of a local casino complex where the car had been found locked and seemingly undamaged. Flip mouthed a silent question and she asked the name of the casino then scribbled it on the piece of paper that was still lying on the table from earlier.

The operator also explained that although they had located the vehicle, entering it or removing it from the parking lot could only be done once the police were present. He also explained that by law they were compelled to report the vehicle recovery to the police, who would ask for the case number as proof that the vehicle owner had reported the vehicle missing.

Reacting to Flip's whispered instructions she explained that with all the shock of the vehicle being stolen right from her yard she had not yet reported the theft to the police. She ended by saying,

" OK, I'll go down to the police station now and open a case. Once I've got the case number I'll phone it through to you."

The operator indicated that this was in order and they would keep the vehicle under surveillance until the police arrived.

Flip suggested that Sannie go to the police station on her own for two reasons: Firstly he needed to go and sort out a few urgent things at work. Secondly there would be those older policemen at the station who would still remember him from his own days on the force. Accompanying the Dominee's wife to report a fairly routine car theft was bound to raise a few eyebrows. Raised eyebrows often lead to curiosity and curiosity would lead to awkward questions.

He left Sannie with an assurance that he would be back soon and strict instructions to call him if she heard anything from the kidnappers.

Flip drove up to the booth and paid the parking fee. He always found it slightly amusing and very sad that the casinos asked for advance payment for parking. That people could be so addicted to gambling they would come out so broke that they could not even afford a few rand for parking astounded him.

He parked his car near the edge of the lot and climbed out. His movements were deliberate and his eyes curious. The parking lot was only about one third full. It was still fairly early in the day and he knew that by nightfall there would not be an empty bay anywhere.

He started from the kerb near the colourful garden that ran just inside the perimeter fence and slowly strolled his way up and down the rows. He hoped the nonchalant aspect, hands in pockets and frequent glances at his watch would give the impression to any onlookers that he was waiting for someone and just killing time by walking around. He was on his eighth row when something caught his subconscious eye. He was not sure at first what it was.

Good police investigators seem to develop a sixth sense about something suspicious or out of place. He glanced around casually. There it was, a small powerful hatchback with tinted windows. Beside it stood a well-built young man wearing aviator sunglasses and a suspicious bulge under his left armpit. It was his rigidity in the midst of casualness that had alerted Flip. Clearly he was here for a purpose. Keeping behind and slightly to one side where he knew he would not be seen he looked in the same direction as the man. It caught his eye almost immediately, Douw's large silver sedan. Obviously this was the surveillance spoken of by the operator at the satellite tracking company.

Flip followed his instincts and a small collection of gamblers into the casino building. He had taken the precaution of stowing his pistol in the small strongbox under the driver's seat of his car. He didn't want the x-ray machine at the entrance to kick up a fuss. Right now he needed to blend in and not be noticed. He did however feel a little bare without a weapon of some sort.

He circled the pit, casually but carefully stalking an as yet identified prey. It took him less than 15 minutes to spot Douw sitting at a blackjack table, a hand of cards held carefully in front of his chest.

A slender blonde sporting plentiful tight curls and an even tighter blouse appeared to be glued to his left arm. She chattered constantly into his ear, clearly excited by the game. When the dealer performed his duty she seemed so overwhelmed with the tension that she tottered on the edge of her chair.

There was no sign of anyone forcing Douw to be where he was, unless the blonde had a secret weapon hidden amongst the generous helping of silicone in her chest.

He glanced around to see if anyone else was watching Douw and saw nothing suspicious. He did however spot a familiar face. Walking up to the elderly security guard in a rumpled uniform who was leaning languidly against a fake corinthian pillar he said,

"Glad to see someone actively involved in the enforcement of law and order"

"Inspector Steyn! Nice to see you. It's been a long time."

"That it has, but it's just plain old Flip Steyn these days. I left the force a while ago."

"And took up gambling instead", came the rather cheeky reply.

Flip smiled at the jibe.

"No, I'm in private security now. Mostly transport and surveillance of valuables."

"Not a lot of valuables in here I'm afraid. You might want to try the pawnshop across the road. A lot of the gamblers transport their valuables in there when their luck and money run out at the same time."

"I see the sense of humour definitely didn't retire."

He was rewarded with a semi-toothy grin.

"No Inspec..er… Mr Steyn."

"You missed your calling George, should have been a stand up comedian."

"No sir, way too much standing from the sound of that."

"Good point. I need your help."

"Any time"

"That gentleman over there, playing blackjack with the bimbo next to him. Has he been here long?"

"Almost non-stop since last night, must have gone home to sleep for a bit and then came straight back early this morning. Seems his luck has changed though."

"How so?"

"Well, a few hours ago he was playing the 50 cent slot machines, looked fairly broke and down on his luck to me. Must have got lucky with one of the one armed bandits when I wasn't looking."

"Or got lucky with one of the ATM's", thought Flip. To the man he said,

"Thanks for your help George, appreciate it as always." They shook hands and as expected his palm was empty of the tightly rolled 50 rand note when their fingers parted. The exchange was so slick and fast, the result of many years' practice on both sides, that it would take a really sharp eye in the control room to spot it on the grainy black and white CCTV monitors.

Flip stood at a slight distance and observed Douw, who remained totally unaware of the attention he was getting from the man half-hidden behind a garish one armed bandit. He was however well aware of the attention he was getting from the less than well-covered blonde on his arm. In between rounds of blackjack they whispered in each other's ears, laughing, smiling and fondling to the point where the pit boss was giving them frequent malevolent glares.

He found the scene repulsive. Douw Pieterse was obviously not being held against his will, although he was being held a great deal by his companion. This man was a church minister yet here he sat deceiving his wife about a kidnapping, gambling away the proceeds and appearing delighted in the company of another woman. A less than impressive woman as well, in Flip's opinion.

Out came the digital camera. With the zoom set at maximum he took a selection of shots of the happy couple. Then he stood waiting to see what would happen next. Waiting for things to happen, sometimes for a very long time, was an activity he had become familiar with during his days as a police detective. Now though he did not have long to wait. Within 20 minutes Douw glanced at his watch, excused himself from the blonde and headed unsteadily for the exit.

Flip followed keeping well out of sight. Douw headed for a quiet part of the parking lot. He took out his cellphone, switched it on and made a call. Once he had finished speaking he glanced at his watch again and went back inside the casino building. Flip stood a while thinking and then followed. He had just passed through the x-ray machine for a second time when his own cellphone rang. He stepped back outside and took the call. It was Sannie explaining the call she had just received. The excitement in her voice was unmistakeable.

"He's free. They let him go. He told me they gave him back his cellphone and are taking him back to his car. I need to clean up and get ready, he'll be here soon. What should I do?"

"If he's on his way back to his car you need to notify the tracking company or they will be suspicious. Probably best to just say it was a big misunderstanding and that he came and fetched the car from home while you were in the shower or something. Give them a description of him and his ID number etc. That way they should believe him when he gets there and there won't be too much fuss."

"I'll do that. Thank you Flip, thank you so much. I'll talk to you later." She rang off leaving Flip staring at the fountain below the stairs.

He decided to wait for Douw to leave the casino. He had a feeling it would not be long. He retrieved his car and moved it to a bay from which he could watch Douw's car while still being far enough away to avoid suspicion. He watched the response officer from the tracking company carefully knowing that he would probably spot Douw first, being that much closer. Flip assumed that by now he would have been briefed by his control room about the latest developments. It was about 30 minutes before the officer stiffened in his seat, climbed out of his car and headed towards Douw's.

An exchange of words followed during which Flip saw Douw show the officer his driver's licence, obviously to identify himself. The officer seemed satisfied with the identification and Douw's explanation. He was allowed to enter and drive away in his car. Flip followed at a distance expecting Douw to head for home. This he did, but only after stopping at the casino entrance to pick up the blonde. On the way to his home Douw pulled in at a townhouse complex, decorated in the customary fake Tuscan kitsch.

Flip was unable to enter without risking been seen, but was able to shoot a hurried photo through the fence while pretending to be strolling down the street. Douw spent only a few minutes in the complex before leaving and heading home. When Flip saw Douw pull into his driveway and Sannie appear at the door he sped up past the house and drove away. Bitterness spread from his mouth throughout his whole body and seeped acidly into his soul. What a hypocrite and liar, he really did not deserve Sannie.

For a moment he was tempted to storm into the house and confront Douw with the photographs in front of Sannie. He decided though that now was not the time or place. Maybe Douw would tell her the truth and they would sort matters out on their own. If not he could show Sannie the photos the next day.

As he drove around aimlessly he began to doubt his first instincts. He had done some really stupid things in his life, some much worse and more devious than what Douw had just done. Being a minister in the constant and critical eye of a congregation was sure to be stressful. Maybe Douw had just snapped and needed to break free for a bit. For all he knew this incident may have just been Douw's way of rebelling and having some fun. Hopefully it was an isolated incident and he had worked whatever it was out of his system. Flip was not sure whether it was worth the heartache to tell his story and destroy Sannie's life and marriage as well as causing embarrassment and hurt to a congregation who obviously looked up to Douw.

He decided, for the time being at least, to do and say nothing. The photos would of course be kept safe in case he felt they were needed.

Life, business and ministry continued as before with barely a mention of the incident for the next three months. Flip was beginning to think he would never need to tell his side of the story. Douw and Sannie, while obviously to him not close, were at least amicable to each other and hospitable to all others. They continued to be respected and loved by the congregation.

Flip was more than ever convinced that he had been right and it was simply an isolated act on Douw's part. Irresponsible and incredibly stupid, but isolated. He was fully prepared to forgive if not quite forget. Until the heat wave that was.

One Sunday morning the congregation sat as usual listening to the ever-forceful Dominee Douw Pieterse deliver a sermon that thundered with righteous anger like a dark cloud and comforted with grace like a silver lining.

Usual as the service was, the weather was unusually hot. The weather service had issued dire warnings to those foolish enough to venture outdoors and proclaimed ominously that this was the worst heat wave in 58 years. As Douw alternately rumbled and smiled from the pulpit the congregation sweated and suffered in the pews. Many a damp, shiny forehead was visible in the rows of the faithful who had risked the ire of the weather service to be in church.

Sannie suffered along with the congregation and Flip glanced across at her frequently, concerned about her paleness. His world spun as she blotted herself with a tissue, accidentally wiping away some of the base on her neck. Just below her right ear a bruise peeked out from below the make-up. In that moment Flip knew that this was not the result of an accident, he just knew.

He had long suspected that Douw had a heavy hand with her but could not prove it. On the one occasion he had raised the subject Sannie had completely denied it and forbidden him from ever mentioning it again.

Now as he sat still with difficulty waiting for the sermon to end, he could not help staring at Douw's large muscular hands as they rained down blows on the defenceless pulpit. How many similar blows had landed on Sannie recently? Flip felt almost violently ill and was about to escape to the bathroom when the service ended.

As usual the congregation filed out slowly, stopping to shake hands and share a few words with Douw and Sannie at the exit. Flip could not bring himself to touch Douw's hand or look Sannie in the eye but instead rushed past, saying he did not feel well and needed some air. He was standing alone in the parking lot when Sannie came up to him to ask if he was all right. He didn't answer her question but said,

"We need to talk, but not here."

"What about, and why not here?"

"Go and look carefully at yourself in the mirror and you'll know why. I'll come to your place after

Douw has left for the church office tomorrow."

Without waiting for her approval he leapt into his car and spattered away. As the gravel settled Sannie's hand went instinctively to the tender spot on her neck.

" Right gentleman, let's get this meeting going. Dominee, would you please open in prayer for us?"

"Thank you Gysie, I'll do that."

Douw smiled at Gysie Van Schalkwyk, one of the congregation's longest serving elders, and bowed his head. The rest of the council of elders followed suit remaining in this posture until Douw's short prayer was finished.

"Amen", pronounced Douw and looked up. As his gaze travelled around the room he saw all the familiar faces except one.

"Does anyone know where Flip Steyn is?"

Nobody answered but a few heads shook to indicate a negative answer.

"Unusual for him to not let me know if he can't make it, I hope everything's all right. I'm sure we'll hear from him later."

This said Douw got into the business of the meeting. Within 90 minutes it was all over.

He walked out into the cool night air and switched on his cellphone with the intention of calling Flip to check if he was all right. Before he could do so the phone played a musical alert tone indicating a message received.

He looked down at the LCD screen that lit up and told him he had three text messages. He opened the new messages folder thinking at least one might be from Flip, explaining his absence from elders meeting. All three messages were from an unfamiliar number.

The first message he opened was an MMS

containing two photo attachments but no message of explanation. His blood chilled as he opened the first photo. It showed him seated at the blackjack table. The next photo was even worse. Not only did it show him gambling but it clearly showed his blonde companion as well, seated so close she might as well have been on his lap.

He was almost afraid to open the next message but his curiosity overcame his fear. Three more photos, showing him leaving the casino with a smile and dropping off the blonde at her home. That time he had not gone in and the final photo was of him driving away.

The photos were date and time stamped so there could be no doubt about when they were taken; the day of the alleged kidnapping. Up till this moment he was convinced his deception had been successful. Sannie had believed his whole explanation and had seemed genuinely pleased that he was home.

As he thought about this he felt guilty about the recent argument which had ended with him losing his temper, slapping her several times and storming out of the house into the arms of the blonde for a few hours. He looked again at the last photo. Who would have done this? The photos were in colour and of a very high quality, not at all the type you would expect from a CCTV recording at a casino. The focus on the pictures was excellent and they showed the subject matter in great detail. Either they had been taken up close, which he doubted, or from a distance by a skilled photographer with a high quality camera.

Was it possible that Sannie had been suspicious and was somehow involved in this? Why then would she have been so welcoming and concerned that he was fine after his ordeal? She had even assured him that the money they had saved for a cruise did not matter as long as he was back safely.

Suddenly it hit him like a hand writing truth in the sand. Flip Steyn. He was a former detective and now a surveillance expert, presumably he was familiar with covert photography. He was also an old and still fairly close friend of Sannie's. Who else had the skills and the personal interest to do something like this? He had often suspected that Flip viewed Sannie with more than just friendship and would be very willing to step into the gap should her marriage ever fail.

So he hadn't been wrong about the look of malice on Sunday after the service, even though Flip had excused it by saying his ulcer was playing up and he was in a bit of pain.

With trepidation he opened the last message, fully expecting it to be a threat from Flip that he was going to Sannie with the information. He was wrong. His world crumbled as he read the short text message.

"Douw, I've been KIDNAPPED…good bye!!!"

Murder on the Platteland Express

Sir Horace Philby squinted at the newspaper spread open before him. A headline proclaiming, *Horse and Trailer Overturn on Busy Freeway*, was the subject of his scrutiny. He looked up at his granddaughter Anne with a question mark shaped frown,

"For goodness sake, why do they allow animals on the freeway in the first place? No wonder there are so many road accidents in South Africa."

Anne turned from the view of Krugersdorp passing by outside and explained, as patiently as she could, that it was not actually a horse that had overturned. It was a truck, also called a mechanical horse. Sir Horace looked at his youngest grandchild with a puzzled look that revealed his still shaky understanding. Anne responded with a half-smile, mentally shaking her head and telling herself that the old boy was really losing it.

Why he had insisted on riding the train to Cape Town instead of flying she really could not fathom. He seemed to be caught up in a world of his own where he believed that trains were romantic and planes just a modern nuisance. Anne much preferred the speed and convenience of flying. As a busy urbanite businesswoman from northern Johannesburg she did not list 26 hours of rattle and shake in a small compartment among her favourite pastimes. They were less than an hour into the journey and she feared it would be a long trip indeed.

Still, she shouldn't complain. It was after all his

money that allowed her to travel to South Africa for the first time during a university break. She had fallen in love with the country and resolved to return as soon as she graduated. This she did and ended up finding a job in Johannesburg and never leaving. Although she enjoyed visiting her family in England once a year she was glad for the opportunity to assert her independence, away from the shadow of her influential relatives.

The train turned its back on greater Johannesburg, broke free from the urban jungle and rolled steadily westwards through an increasingly rural landscape. Anne snuggled into the corner of the bench seat and stared into the darkening scenery. Soon the sun would set and it would be too dark to see anything. Not that there would be much to see as the scenery smoothed out into the flat and yellow rural *Platteland* of South Africa's interior. After a short while the motion of the train and her tiredness took effect and she dozed off, leaving Sir Horace to his newspaper.

Seemingly within seconds, although she knew it must have been much longer, Anne's sleep was disturbed by the steward's insistent rap on the door. She rose from her seat and opened the door.

"Excuse me Miss, we will be serving dinner shortly. Please make your way to the dining car when you are ready."

Anne noticed that her grandfather was asleep in his seat, the newspaper still spread open before him. Not even the knock on the door and the subsequent conversation had awakened him.

"If you don't mind I think we will come along a little later."

"No problem, just don't leave it too late."

As the steward left Anne contemplated the scenery outside. It was nearly dark but the surroundings were visible in a vague, silhouetted way. The train was making its way across a broad flat plain that offered very little by way of relief. She consulted her timetable and decided they must be nearing Potchefstroom, place of education of many leaders of the *apartheid* regime and first settler town north of the Vaal River. The desire for sleep had abated somewhat and she was getting hungry but Anne decided to allow her grandfather to continue sleeping for another fifteen minutes or so before waking him for dinner.

Once in the dining car Anne scouted for a place to sit. The only available seating was to be opposite a rather strange looking young man who was eating alone. He seemed to consist of little more than skinny limbs, a large baggy T-shirt and an enormous mop of wild blonde hair. He ate mechanically while absorbed in the contents of a surfing magazine. Oh well, there was nowhere else to sit so better make the most of it. Beckoning to her grandfather to follow her she approached the table.

"Hi, mind if we join you?"

"Hey no prob, fill the seat up with yourself", came the reply from across the table. Anne and Sir Horace seated themselves, Sir Horace staring distastefully at the casual untidiness of the young man opposite.

My name is Anne", she said by way of introduction, "and this is my grandfather, Sir Horace Philby".

"Howzit, I'm Bruce" was the reply.

The mention of the title Sir appeared to have stirred Bruce temporarily out of his interest in the magazine, so much so that he actually put down the publication, stopped slouching and sat up straight as he stared at Sir Horace.

"Are you, like a real knight?"

"I was knighted by Her Majesty the Queen some years ago, yes."

"Wicked *bru*", said Bruce, impressed.

Although Sir Horace was not sure what wickedness had to do with his title, much less what bru meant, he decided to remain silent and allow Anne to do the talking.

His curiosity in Sir Horace satisfied, surfer-boy returned to burying his head in the magazine.

An officious looking man clad in a white jacket and black trousers approached their table. Evidently he was the waiter.

"Good evening, my name is Schalk. May I fetch you something to drink?"

"Skulk", repeated Sir Horace to himself, not sure if he liked the sound of that. Rather devious sounding. Anne could see by the slightly glazed look in her grandfather's eyes that he had gone off at a mental tangent. Wearily she looked around for something to occupy her attention.

Seated at the next table were Hennie and Hettie Duvenhage. Hettie was a woman of prodigious cooking talents. She also belonged to the old school of thought which maintained that, "The way to a man's heart is through his stomach". If this was true, Hettie had her work cut out. In Hennie's case the route to his heart would be an arduous one owing to his substantial girth and fussy eating habits.

Currently Hennie was eyeing with suspicion the latest offering from the cramped kitchen aboard the train, *Chicken a la Microwave*. There was a more glamorous name on the menu and truthfully it wasn't that bad but such was Hennie's dislike of hastily prepared food that he could not think of it any other way.

At a table near the far end of the coach sat a

solitary, slightly morose looking man. Anne guessed
he was in his mid thirties, which made it a little more
unusual for him to be travelling alone than Bruce who
was still very young and footloose.

Looking at him more closely Anne concluded he
was some sort of artistic type. A gaudy ethnic-print
shirt hung over jeans that had the appearance of a
long and chequered life. Leather sandals decorated
with coloured beads completed the outfit. Anne
thought he would have fitted in better in the sixties
and made a fine hippie.

Unremarkable people occupied the rest of the
tables. A few couples, some small family groups;
mostly average middle-class types. From the
unfamiliar words that floated to her ears occasionally
Anne surmised that at least some of them were
foreign tourists.

One couple did catch her eye for a few moments.
The man sat with his attention focused on the glass
before him, paying absolutely no attention to his wife
who stared over his shoulder at the television
mounted high on a bracket at the end of the coach.
Judging from his unsteady slumped look, the glass
had been re-filled several times during dinner. How
was it that people who presumably had enough
passion for each other at some stage to want to marry
ended in this state a decade or two later.

She was glad she was single and self-sufficient, for
the time being at least. Maybe one day she would
meet the right man and want to domesticate a little,
but she certainly never wanted to end up in the shoes
of the couple staring in opposite directions.

They ordered and ate: Sir Horace fish and she
chicken. During dinner the occupants of the car
engaged in desultory conversation or glanced out of
the windows between mouthfuls. Klerksdorp

appeared alongside, houses blinked briefly at the train and disappeared.

As the tables began to empty some of the train staff moved through the car clearing away cutlery and crockery. Later the lights would be dimmed, some of the tables collapsed away against the walls and the coach would double as a bar.

Anne had no intention of spending the evening in a mobile drinking facility and she was sure that Sir Horace would want an early night. As soon as they were finished with after-dinner coffee she suggested they return to the compartment and see if there was anything worthwhile on the small television.

As they walked down the slightly rocking passage she noticed the woman from earlier entering a compartment, alone. Presumably her husband had elected to stay and patronise the bar a little, or maybe a lot.

When she and Sir Horace entered their own compartment she saw that the folding bench seats had already been converted into beds and made up with linen and blankets.

After her grandfather had brushed his teeth she slipped into the bathroom that was little bigger than a large wardrobe to take a shower, leaving Sir Horace to change into pajamas and prepare for bed.

By the time she emerged, all warm and freshly scrubbed, his snoring was giving the TV soundtrack some competition. She decided there was nothing to watch that appealed to her and turned it off.

The small reading light above the bed was more than adequate so she settled under the covers with a magazine and spent a happy hour or so reading about the scandalous lives of the rich and famous.

Soon her eyelids were fighting a losing battle with gravity and she snapped off the light switch. She released the spring-loaded window blind so it scooted up in its frame.

The view outside was amazing. The full moon was staring down at the flat expanse of farmland and a pale shine reflected off fields of wheat that swayed in a gentle breeze. Anne fell asleep with her head in a pool of moonlight.

She narrowly missed the awesome sight of the moon's smile reflected whitely off the gentle waters of the Bloemhof dam. While she slept the train stepped out and cantered through the landscape passing the small towns of Christiana and Warrenton with barely a glance. Kimberly, home to the famous Big Hole, warranted a brief stop an hour or so after midnight.

She woke early, just as the darkness of the sky was being tinted with a pinkness that promised a spectacular sunrise. The view out of the uncurtained window was so serene and uncluttered that Anne simply swung her legs out of the bed and sat leaning against the wall watching the mostly rural countryside clickity-clack past. She looked with interest as the huge locomotive and rolling stock graveyard passed by. She had heard of this place and correctly decided that they were passing the Northern Cape town of De Aar.

Sitting like this she had to concede that travelling by train had its merits. No busy airport terminal and rushing crowds to contend with. No sitting in cramped seats staring at the dandruff-riddled head in front of you. Having dinner at a table off proper plates instead of a plastic tray on your lap felt so much classier.

Her grandfather may be a little senile and odd in his ways but he might be right about the train idea. Unless you were travelling for business and needed to reach your destination in the shortest possible time the train made travelling much more of an experience than flying. She glanced over to the bunk opposite where the old man slept wrapped in flannel and dreams of a full and interesting life.

Not long after dawn the steward rapped gently at the door to inform her that breakfast was available if she was interested. She decided to sit a while longer and have a late breakfast with Sir Horace. From the shuffling sounds in the passage outside it seemed the majority of passengers had opted for an early breakfast. Good, that way there would be less of a crowd a little later. Anne returned to the view and her thoughts.

As she sat thus contemplating the passing countryside and occasionally Sir Horace, Anne noticed the train slowing down. At first she thought it was her imagination but as she looked out the window it was obvious that they were not moving at quite the same pace as before.

This realisation was confirmed by a grating squeal from the wheels as the driver applied the brakes. In common with the few other passengers who still occupied their compartments and the majority who occupied the dining car, she wondered why the train was making an unscheduled stop. Surely Beaufort-West was still some way off.

The train stopped at a small unknown halt in the midst of flat unspectacular scenery and curious passengers observed a yellow bakkie with police badges on both doors standing to one side. Their curiosity was further stimulated by the slightly rotund and balding figure that removed himself from the passenger seat and climbed aboard the train. He entered the coach directly behind the twin electric locomotives. Almost immediately the train resumed its journey.

Within minutes those passengers still in their compartments began receiving requests from train staff to assemble in the dining car as soon as possible. No explanation was offered as to the reason for this assembly.

Anne woke her grandfather as gently as possible and explained the situation. It was obvious that Sir Horace was not fully awake and did not quite comprehend what he was being told, but he pulled an overcoat over his pajamas and followed her out of the compartment without resistance.

As Anne and Sir Horace made their way slowly along the corridor, other passengers could be seen moving in the same direction. Some moved quietly and without complaint, others demanded to know why such a strange request had been made of them without explanation. These demands appeared to fall on ears that if not actually deaf were at least hard of hearing. All they received was a stiff assurance that an explanation would be forthcoming once everybody was assembled.

In the dining car the occupants of the train arranged themselves as best they could around the gently swaying room. Although it was a little crowded, all of them were accommodated fairly well. The train was nowhere near full, presumably because it was a mid-week trip. Anne noticed the man who had left the police vehicle earlier and climbed on to the train standing near the door at the far end of the coach. As soon as it appeared everyone was present he stepped forward, cleared his throat to gain attention and spoke,

"Good Morning Ladies and Gentleman, I am Detective Inspector Jakobus Verband of the South African Police Service. I am sure you all want to

know why I needed to speak to you here this morning.
Well I will come right to the point. I am not a man
known for beating around the bush. I do not mince
words. I call a spade a spade. I tell it as I see it. I do
not..."

He was cut short by the hippie sighing loudly and
asking, "Could you get on with it, some of us have
lives to lead and its time for breakfast." The inspector
aimed a frozen look in the direction from which the
comment had come,

"As I was saying before I was interrupted, it is
alleged that a crime, a serious crime were committed
on this train last night. A passenger is alleged to have
disappeared without trace and apparently without the
train having stopped."

The emphasis that he placed on the words alleged
and apparently indicated to all present, except
possibly Hennie who was eyeing the closed kitchen
door with suspicion, that he had his doubts and did
not enjoy being assigned to this case.

Anne saw the unhappily married woman standing
meekly to one side, trails of teary moisture on her
cheeks. She was alone and it seemed likely that her
husband was the missing man. The inspector's next
sentence confirmed this.

"Mrs Terblanche reported that her husband, Mr
Brian Terblanche, was missing this morning when she
woke and did not appear to have come to bed last
night."

The inspector glanced towards Mrs Terblanche
with what seemed to Anne a slightly accusatory look
then held up a photograph and continued;

"I have here a photo of Mr Terblanche that was
kindly supplied by his wife. I will show it to all of
you as and when we speak. If you remember seeing
anything to do with the man in it please let me know

as soon as possible. I will remain on the train for most of today while it continues towards Cape Town. During the day I will need to ask some questions of everyone on the train and I request your fullest co-operation."

This said he sat down. Gradually the dining car returned to a state of near normality. Those who had arrived earlier returned to their breakfasts and some of the others decided to eat as they were already in the dining car. The talk at every table centred on the Inspector's speech. Every table that was except the last in the corner. This table was occupied by a surfing magazine behind which slouched the rather untidy form of Bruce Stevens, completely oblivious to the events happening around him.

Inspector Verband noticed the inattention of this lone passenger, moved over to the table and seated himself opposite Bruce. "Excuse me Sir", he said in a tone of voice which indicated how lightly he used the term Sir

"Did you hear what I was just saying?"

The magazine lowered and Bruce looked at the Inspector in surprise.

" Sorry bru, I was like just checking out the pics of J-Bay, wicked surf hey", replied Bruce turning the magazine to show the Inspector the article he was reading.

"*Ja*, very nice, but about the disappearance of Mr Terblanche", continued the Inspector, dragging a reluctant notebook and pencil from his pocket, Did you notice anything suspicious about his behaviour or the behaviour of any other persons on the train?"

Bruce looked at the inspector with a puzzled look on his face, "Nought, you mean Brian has just like disappeared? And you can't find him anywhere?"

"That are the usual meaning of disappeared",

muttered Verband, characteristically confusing the plural and singular. "Did you notice anything suspicious or unusual?"

"Hey not really bru, except that he was like half-*dronk* when he got on the train. Looked like he had a mean amount of *dop* in his case as well."

"You mean that Mr Terblanche was under the influence of alcohol when he boarded the train?" repeated Verband.

"Ja, that's what I said", acknowledged Bruce.

"And furthermore that there was a large amount of alcoholic drink concealed in his luggage?

"Ja bru."

The Inspector removed a pen and notebook from his pocket and prepared to take notes. "I'll need a statement from you. What are your full name?"

"Bruce Alan Stevens", was the reply from beneath the mop of bleached hair across the table.

"Occupation?"

"Student."

"Home address?"

"12 Bayview road, Observatory, Cape Town."

Verband recorded Bruce's telephone details and identity number, and left the table adding,

"I may need to ask you further questions later, please keep yourself available." He then left Bruce to continue his earlier pastime and moved off to question some of the other passengers.

Next in line to observe the Inspector's questioning skills was the man Anne could not help thinking of as the hippie. As Verband seated himself at the table eyes rose and regarded him with slight irritation. It was clear to all but the most dim-witted observer (in this case Hennie) that Mike regarded the entire process as a colossal waste of time.

"What about you Sir? Did you have any contact with the allegedly missing person, a Mr (the inspector consulted his notes briefly), Brian Terblanche?"

"I think I may have passed him in the corridor, didn't pay him much attention."

"I see. Well if I can just get your particulars in case I need you further…"

This request of the Inspector's was met with a sigh. Pretending not to notice the rudeness and impatience he began his laborious gathering of information.

"Full name?"

"Michael John Payne. "

"Occupation?"

"Freelance artistic entrepreneur."

"Meaning?"

"Meaning exactly what I said Inspector!"

The inspector countered Mike's withering glare with a blank stare.

"Ja, OK. But it's not really a recognised profession. Is this how you make your living?"

"Yes. I make a living from a variety of pursuits: painting, specialised bead work, Feng Shui consulting and a few others."

Inspector Verband bit the end of his pen and mentally grappled with Feng Shui, a phrase he had never heard before. He eventually gave up and just wrote unemployed.

Mike spotted this. His lips firmed into a hard horizontal line and a fire started to flicker somewhere just behind his eyes.

"I am NOT unemployed inspector, I made that perfectly clear."

"Ja, but it's not really a real job is it."

The animosity was now flowing in both directions.

" For your information inspector, I hold a degree in political science. I do not do what I do because I'm uneducated, stupid and can't find a real job. I do it because I enjoy it!"

The inspector's eyebrows reached for the sky, giving the impression that he did not regard political science as a real education anyway.

This gesture poured fuel on the fire, causing a verbal explosion.

" Frankly Inspector, I find your attitude towards free-thinking artists offensive. You seem determined to stereotype all of us as decadent layabouts, interested only in liberal politics and sins of the flesh. I choose not to waste my talent or education in the fruitless pursuit of material wealth and slave endlessly at the coalface of capitalistic greed. Just because I am not a part of your conservative Calvinistic world with all its *verkrampte* values and beliefs you categorise me as an overeducated bum!"

This eloquent tirade over, he sat back and dug in his shirt pocket for a few seconds, producing with a flourish a dilapidated packet of cigarettes. The flourish was somewhat marred by the fact that he also dislodged a well-worn unemployment card, which fluttered down to land beside his leg on the vinyl seat.

The sight of the card, the challenging stare from Mike and the less challenging but still disconcerting stares of a coach full of curious onlookers had the effect of causing Inspector Verband to look both uncomfortable and violently angry at once. Fortunately his violent, embarrassed demeanour led to nothing more than him stalking angrily from the coach, dark mutterings scattering in his wake.

" Hey bru looks like you like seriously hacked off the inspector", commented Bruce from a far corner of the coach. For once he appeared to have found the world around him more interesting than his usual pursuit of reading surfing magazines.

"I need a smoke", was the only response, flung over Mike's shoulder as he exited the coach.

After the peak of animosity, activity in the dining car dipped into a trough of stunned silence and then slowly recovered until a muted buzz of curious dialogue could be heard emanating from several points around the coach. All of those present were speculating on the reason for Mike's vociferous outburst. All except Hennie of course who was speculating on the emptiness of both his plate and his stomach, being generally accustomed to more robust meals.

As conversation in the dining car ebbed and flowed cautiously, Mike made his way to his shared compartment in the second class section of the train. The two other occupants of the half-full compartment were absent. In common with most of the passengers, they were in the dining car. Inspector Verband walked aimlessly along the passage, having no compartment to call his own.

The rest of the morning passed smoothly enough. It was not exactly peaceful, more a state of truce. The knowledge that a man had disappeared and the simmering tension between Mike and the inspector created a mood of quiet discomfort.

The passengers moved about the train as they pleased. Inspector Verband also moved about questioning passengers and staff as he encountered them. The train seemed the only unaffected party, clicking and rolling its way towards Cape Town as was its twice-weekly custom.

Shortly after noon those who had opted for an early lunch, the inspector among them, sparsely populated the dining car. During the meal some passengers noticed the train manager and a steward come to talk to the inspector who immediately left with the two men. A few people heard mention of a body and the whispered rumour spread like voracious flames. Some of the more curious souls present left the car and headed down the passage in the same direction as the inspector.

The party of three stopped in front of a door pointed out by the steward. He stepped forward, tugged on a light chain that ran from his belt loop into his trouser pocket and used the resulting key to unlock the door. He moved out of the way and nodded to the inspector.

Inspector Verband took hold of the handle, opened the door a crack and looked inside. Several others looked over his shoulder with caution, including the more curious of the passengers. The sight within sucked a hiss of breath from most of those present. Inside the closet the slumped body of a man lay half-covered in a shower of assorted linen and bedding. A further and more intense collective hiss occurred when the body stirred slightly. A female voice screamed and was stifled. Verband yanked the door open.

Brian Terblanche squinted in the sudden inflow of light and observed the small knot of onlookers with bleary puzzlement. He attempted to sit upright but only succeeded in dislodging more of the contents of the narrow shelves. Blankets, sheets and pillows cascaded down and buried him like a woven and knitted avalanche. Several helpful hands reached forward and dug him out.

He looked again at the faces observing him and tried to work out where he was. Dim recollections started to emerge from a distant part of his alcohol-soaked brain. Memories of staggering down the passage and opening the door to what he assumed was his room swam through the hangover and into his conscious mind. He could not remember anything after he stumbled through the doorway. There was a vague image of waking several times and attempting to fight his way out of a small, dark and seemingly padded room. At first he thought he was remembering a bad dream but then looked around at his surroundings and concluded he was remembering snatches of a confused and rather terrifying night.

On his way to bed after a long evening spent in the company of potstill brandy and a window behind which the landscape rushed giddily by, he had mistaken the door to a linen closet for that of his compartment a few metres away. As he stumbled inside his forehead collided with the edge of a shelf. The mixture of alcohol, pain and shock was too much for his constitution and he fainted.

Aside from a few dizzy wakeful moments during which he beat feebly on the door, which had by now been locked by one of the stewards, he spent the next 12 hours lying asleep on the floor of the closet. Eventually one of the train staff who was tasked with making beds opened the door to get a fresh load of linen and was horrified to find what she assumed to be a corpse inside. Her scream of fright brought one of the stewards running. He re-locked the door and quickly called the train manager.

Brian was now helped to his unsteady feet by the inspector and a few curious witnesses that were beginning to assemble in ever-increasing numbers in the passage. Verband quickly took charge and dismissed the curious faces, telling them that they would all be informed as soon as the situation had been clarified.

Brian, his wife and the inspector entered the

Terblanche's cabin. Presumably Brian would now face some questioning from Verband, and quite possibly from Mrs Terblanche as well

The small crowd dispersed in a cloud of excited chatter and speculation. The news that Brian Terblanche had been found alive if not very well ran up and down the train. Many opinions were voiced and rumours spread, but after a short while the excitement of the moment faded and the passengers returned to their previous activities, either in the dining car or their compartments.

Anne and Sir Horace had not been present during Brian's discovery and came to hear of it from fellow passengers during their own later lunch. While the juicy gossip flowed around the dining car the dry town of Laingsburg passed by outside. Hard to believe that an unexpected and catastrophic flood occurred in such a barren place in the 80's.

After lunch they retired to the compartment to relax and read a bit, Sir Horace the daily paper and Anne a travel guide. She found it fun to read about a town as the train passed through. She learnt that Matjiesfontein was famous for being the birthplace of South African author Olive Schreiner and for the Lord Milner Hotel, one of the few surviving examples of Victorian architecture in South Africa.

Inspector Verband called a meeting in the dining car at 15H00. As this coincided with afternoon teatime most passengers were already present and only a few had to be summoned from their rooms by the stewards. The inspector explained to all that Mr Terblanche had fortunately been found unharmed. He did not go into detail about how and where he was found or how he came to be there, simply announcing that the situation was resolved and they should all forget about it and enjoy what was left of the journey.

Ann packed quickly and efficiently then sat by the window to enjoy the remainder of the trip. The shadows began to lengthen as the train passed through the picturesque towns of Worcester and Wellington in the magnificent Cape Winelands region.

Eventually the line snaked away from the N1 freeway that it had mirrored for much of the journey and ran through the small town of Huguenot. The train avoided the Hottentots Holland Mountains that stood across the way to Cape Town while the freeway burrowed through them via the Huguenot Tunnel.

An hour later the train squealed into Cape Town station. The passengers alighted and scattered while the train staff busily made arrangements for Inspector Verband to be on the train the next day when it headed for Johannesburg on the return journey. For the time being he was left standing on the empty platform with only his thoughts for company, dark thoughts of odd passengers and drunken idiots!

The Tall One

Jane stood nervously on the edge and gazed down at the majestic Howick Falls, Nogqaza the Zulu call it - The Tall One. She looked over the lip at the kilolitres of water plummeting down into the abysmal pool below, a river plucked from meandering by gravity and hurled, boiling and frothing, over the cliff.

Standing on the rocky parapet Jane sensed the phenomenon that made some people feel compelled to throw themselves over the edge of a cliff. Perhaps the accident that had claimed the ferryman's son all those years ago had not been so accidental after all. Perhaps the young man had felt compelled to release the bridle, slip off his mount and drift with the current over the edge. Maybe the subject of the first recorded death at the falls actually wanted to fly from the cliff and leave the world behind.

Looking into the large pool at the base of the falls surrounded by a myriad of lesser minions, she reflected how cool and inviting the water looked.

Jane resisted the urge to leap and instead retraced her steps to the car park, knowing that she would return soon. The majesty and mystery of the place had struck a hook deep into her soul. Howick is by no means the greatest of the country's falls, but few others are as steeped in lore and legend. From rumours and legends of fearsome reptilian inhabitants to new-age assertions of convergent ley lines, the place has a slightly ethereal quality that belies its close proximity to the national route from Durban to Johannesburg a scant handful of kilometres away. The

Zulu revere it as a place of magic, the tourists and day-trippers flock to it out of curiosity, varying measures of awe and photo opportunities.

As she climbed into her car, Jane was conscious of all these mingled forces and emotions. Driving back to her home in Durban she pondered the turmoil in her life that had driven her to the top of the falls, with the urge to leap hastily but barely suppressed.

She was sexually molested at 10 by an uncle and then raped at 12 by an older cousin, the son of the same uncle. With her innocent femininity battered and shredded by the harsh reality of incestuous lust, she had slipped into a destructive whirlpool of cursory, numerous and short lived sexual encounters with a multitude of initially physically and later mentally adolescent men.

Eventually, having walked a long and bitter road of forced maturity that exceeded her physical years, she decided in her mid twenties that her life in its misshapen form was not worth living; in fact it wasn't worth much at all.

The bottle of prescription painkillers in the bathroom cabinet served as a gateway to eternity. Fortunately (or maybe unfortunately from her point of view), the gate was firmly closed just in time by a concerned friend. Unsettled by the unanswered telephone Michelle, friend and sometime confidant to Jane, had come to the flat on a hunch. The hunch proved correct and Jane was carefully, if reluctantly, pulled back into consciousness by a medical team at the local hospital.

Many times in the next few years Jane resented the intervention. Whenever her mind was at a tempestuous summit of negative emotion, she told herself that she should have been dead. If it hadn't been for Michelle her problems would have been over.

The experience of standing at the top of the falls had produced a profound effect within her psyche. The majesty, power and atmosphere of the place had struck deep into her core and she resolved to return to complete the experience.

A seed of necessity had been planted in her heart and she needed to water it. As she drove away she felt something break within her and knew that she must return to put an end to the pulsating hurt.

Another bright and unreal day several weeks later Jane was back at the falls gazing into the water. The surface reflected her face; the dark depths seemed to reflect her soul. She gathered her courage, shoved her trepidation aside and threw herself from the rock.

Down she travelled, feeling the crisp coolness of the water and the shock. Down, down then reversing and floating back up to the surface of the pool into which she had leapt, bursting from the watery cocoon in an explosion of spray and bubbles.

The bottom of the falls was much less frightening than the top, but no less intriguing. It was over, finally over - washed away by the cathartic natural power of the place. The road would be long, but for the first time she had the will to walk it

Aliens

"Miss Voyant, welcome. We've heard a lot about you and are delighted to have you here with us."

"Thank you very much, but please call me Claire."

The lodge manager smiled at the young woman. He had initially had some reservations about taking a booking for a paranormal convention, especially on the same weekend as a prominent bank's annual conference. He had half-expected the convention organiser to be an old hag in a black cape, possibly with a pet bat or something. The thought of some freaky witch-types mixing with a collection of conservative bankers was a little disturbing.

To his surprise Claire seemed very normal and sweet. Hopefully the rest of the delegates were as nice. She was a minor local celebrity after helping the police solve some high-profile murder and kidnapping cases. Having her host a convention at the lodge was good publicity.

He surveyed the reception area that was filled with a mixed and milling group of people that seemed to swell by the minute. Paranormal delegates, bankers and local tourists up for the weekend all blended into an excited chattering troop. The sight of several game-viewing vehicles outside and the notice near the door advertising lion feeding created an expectant atmosphere amongst the guests, many of whom were hoping to see lots of game up close during their stay. The private game reserve and lodge was a popular destination for locals and foreign tourists alike, despite its fairly remote location.

Some of the locals had braved the 5 ½ hour drive from Johannesburg. Others, along with most of the foreign tourists, had elected to fly into nearby Musina and then be collected by the lodge shuttle service and driven the last 90 kilometres or so.

After checking in most of the guests went to their rooms to unpack and in some cases change their clothing. Within an hour many of them had returned to the main building and were drifting about in the bar or out on the deck enjoying the sunset over the nearby waterhole.

The sight and smell of large skewers filled with chunks of venison and other meats spitting and popping over an open fire whipped appetites to a frenzy. With relief and excitement the guests flowed into the dining room when the manager announced that the dinner serving was about to begin. Kitchen staff circulated around the room waving the skewers like clumsy swords and pried off various cuts, both wild and domestic, as requested by each guest.

The buzz of conversation subsided as the room collectively settled down to the business of consuming large quantities of meat and associated trimmings. Here and there soft voices could be heard but most mouths were occupied with eating.

As the meal neared an end one guest caught the roving manager's attention and asked fairly loudly,

"Excuse me. We saw something about lion feeding on a sign. When does it happen? We'd like to see it."

The manager raised his voice, as he believed many of the guests would be interested in the answer,

"We feed the lions either on a Saturday or Sunday, depending on how many guests are in the lodge", answered the manager.

A burst of laughter from a table near the window

intruded on the conversation.

"So when the lodge gets a bit crowded you thin the guests out by feeding them to the lions hey."

In unison all the occupants of the room looked towards the speaker. A large florid man wrapped in khaki sat slapping the table and laughing with enthusiasm at his own joke. Next to him his wife laughed along, her shrill cackle quickly overshadowing his throatier guffaw. He was a large noisily cheerful looking man while she was an absolute vision of kitsch; all fake leopard skin, fake blondeness and fake cleavage. The kind of person that is hard to ignore. Love her, hate her, and threaten to deprive her of plastic surgery maybe, but certainly not walk past without a second look. The look of misunderstanding on the manager's face convinced the joker to abandon any further attempts at humour.

As the evening wore on the guests slowly dispersed, some directly to their rooms and the rest scattering themselves between the bar and adjacent wooden deck or the reading lounge that led off the reception area.

The next morning dawned cool and clear with a blue sky already tinged with a warning shimmer of rising heat later in the day. Guests trickled in for breakfast, the conference and convention attendees first as they had a schedule to keep, the tourists later and at a more leisurely pace. At a corner table sat a lone banker, appearing slightly out of his element in casual clothes and with a green and brown vista before him instead of the usual Sandton skyline.

He consumed a sensible helping of muesli, yoghurt and chopped fruit and then stood up to go look for something more exciting. Bacon and eggs maybe, let the doctor's advice go unheeded for once As he was poking around the breakfast buffet a large form approached him with a muscular hand firmly outstretched. It was the same man who had made the silly joke the previous evening about feeding guests to the lions.

"Boet Erasmus", boomed an introduction, "and this is my wife Cherie"

"Mike, Mike Watson", he answered in return.

"So Mike Mike Watson, you here on business or pleasure?"

"A bit of both actually. Here on a conference but looking forward to squeezing in a bit of game viewing if I can."

"Nothing wrong with a bit of a squeeze." Mike groaned as Boet slapped his wife's buttocks. The man was obviously convinced he was a major comedic talent.

"So Mike, what business are you in?"

"Banking."

"Sounds like fun."

Mike grimaced slightly at the sarcasm, but decided to be polite anyway.

"And yourself Boet, what do you do for a living?"

"We're in the meat business, own a wholesaler in Pretoria East."

"Interesting. Please excuse me, I need to finish up here. We have our first session starting soon."

"Ja, fine. Have a *lekker* time, don't work too hard now."

Mike moved away to eat his bacon and eggs, drink coffee, and quickly scan the newspaper headlines. He was sure Boet Erasmus meant well and was only trying to be friendly but he was rather overpowering and loud. The dining room emptied as the business guests went to join their relevant conference or convention and those there for pleasure wandered off, either to relax in and around the lodge or to go explore the reserve.

The small wooden jetty squealed in protest as a large man thumped along it towards the tiny office near the end. He stopped and surveyed the sign above the small rustic counter with interest.

Aerial Game Viewing / Lunch on the Dam
R300 pp
Enjoy a unique view over the reserve and
surrounding countryside followed by lunch
in the middle of the dam on a private island

While Bill Austin studied the sign with interest the attendant behind the counter regarded him with faint curiosity. Gaudy shirt, jeans, leather belt with a large metal buckle sporting two wild mustangs, cowboy boots - all topped off with an enormous stetson hat. He looked like an American tourist. This assumption proved to be correct when he spoke,

"How y'all doing? So tell me about this here trip. You use a boat or a plane or what?" The burst of Texan accent rang and echoed over the water.

"Actually a bit of both. We use that." The attendant pointed to an amphibious airplane moored slightly offshore.

"First it flies over the reserve then lands in the middle of the dam next to the island where a picnic lunch will be served."

"Sounds good, give me two tickets. When does it leave?"

"We usually wait till there are four passengers to fill the plane and then it leaves. So far we have three. If nobody else arrives in the next 20 minutes or so it will take off anyway. You can wait over there and enjoy the view if you like." He nodded in the direction of a few wooden benches under a thatched shelter.

"Great, we'll do that."

Bill paid for two tickets then tramped towards the shelter at the end of the jetty, his wife Sally following silently in his shadow as usual. They stepped into the semi-darkness and realised there was a quiet woman sitting in the corner. She greeted them with a soft but distinctive German accent. The three settled into a companionable silence and regarded the still beauty before them. The plane rocked gently on the water, the relaxed form of the pilot vaguely visible through the glare from the windscreen.

Inside the cockpit David Sanders dozed in the hot air. A veteran rural pilot, his antics as a young crop duster earned him the nickname "Crazy Dave." This name had followed him for almost 30 years but was of course never used in the presence of tourists.

The scene remained unchanged for ten minutes or so until more footsteps could be heard on the planking leading to the office. All the occupants of the shelter looked up. A large impressive camera lens appeared to be dragging a hapless Asian-looking man towards them. The lens and its prisoner stopped at the counter, read the sign and engaged the attendant in conversation. A short dialogue followed which was punctuated by hand signals and carefully enunciated English words. Ticket bought, the Asian man joined the party of three under the shelter. The man from the office followed him in.

" OK ladies and gentlemen. We have our party of four. Please make your way to the stairs over there and climb into the boat at the bottom. Morris here will ferry you out to the plane and see you safely aboard."

An as yet unnoticed man stepped into the thatched

shadow and flashed them a shy smile. The four tourists clambered into the boat with lots of stumbling and helping hands. In contrast Morris leaped from the second last step and landed lightly in the stern. The boat pulled away from its mooring under power of a small electric motor and puttered towards the plane.

Bill Austin was looking unnaturally pale and very uncomfortable. Morris wondered just how this large noisy man would handle the flight, including a waterborne takeoff and landing when the light chop on the river was making him seasick.

"You OK sir?"

"I'm fine, just feeling the heat."

Obviously he was not going to admit weakness in public, more bravado than common sense.

The boat pulled alongside the plane, gonging gently into one of the hollow metal pontoons that kept it afloat. The word *Goni* was painted onto one of the metal surfaces. Bill, ever curious, asked loudly,

"Say, what does that mean?"

Morris was a local man who belonged to the Venda nation. As such he was a second-language English speaker. He scratched his head slightly and replied,

"Actually sir, I don't know the English word. It's Tshivenda for a bird that flies high in the sky then crashes into the water."

This last point he illustrated by slapping the fist of one hand into the open palm of the other. Accurate as his description of a fish eagle was, it did not help Bill Austin's fragile state and caused him to turn a paler shade of green.

"Ah well, I'm not sure if I feel up to this after all. Feeling the heat you see."

"You want me to take you and your wife back?"

"I'd still like to go Bill, if I can." said Mrs Sally

Austin, uncharacteristically expressing an opinion.

Bill looked slightly taken aback for a moment but recovered quickly and said,

"Sure darlin, if it's what you want. I can go back to the lodge and come back later to pick you up"

"Sir, I can get one of the lodge drivers to take madam back if you want."

"Why thank you kindly. Tell you what, keep my ticket money and let these here folks go have a good time. I'll go back to the lodge and rest a little. Sure I'll be as right as rain in no time. Don't want to take any chances. We're booked to go see Mugabe tomorrow. Would hate to miss it 'cos I'm feelin' poorly."

Morris looked up, impressed,

"You have an appointment with President Mugabe?"

"President…"

Bill Austin and Morris faced each other through a haze of misunderstanding.

"Mugabe, the mountain with the old ruins…"

"Oh, Mapungubwe", said Morris with a good-natured chuckle.

"That's it. The one where they found the golden elephant."

"Rhino."

"Huh, where?"

"It was a golden rhino sir. At Mapungubwe."

"Yeah OK, I guess you are right. You'd best get these folks on board now. Just make sure Mrs Austin gets back safe and sound after the trip."

"Sure Sir. I'll take you back now as soon as they are in the plane."

A short while later the small boat headed back to shore while the plane taxied down the widening river and into the open water of the dam. David Sanders looked into the middle distance to check for obstructions and then gunned the motor. The aircraft pushed heavily through the water for a few seconds and then rose up on its pontoons as if tiptoeing. It picked up speed, bumping and slapping over the surface until the water rushed underneath in a muddy blur.

Sanders pulled the yoke back and the plane lifted off the surface with the propeller clawing and scrabbling for height in the thin heated air. Like most of South Africa's interior, the northernmost Limpopo province is situated at fairly high altitude. He banked over the lake and swept the plane around in a gentle arc until yellow savannah appeared below. The engine caught its breath and mumbled into a dull drone as the throttle was pulled back. Sanders picked up his radio handset and made contact with some of the game rangers on the ground. He used the information that came back to adjust his course and head for the area where the highest concentrations of game had been spotted.

Within minutes the three tourists on board caught sight of mixed herds of various antelope, zebra and wildebeest. A buzz of excitement crackled through the cabin as wide-eyed faces were pressed to windows for a better look. Sanders took the plane into a shallow dive and went as low and close as he could without panicking the animals and risking a collision with some of the taller trees.

Sally Austin gazed out of the window in wonderment, the German lady sat with her palms pressed tight against her knees and the expression on her face see-sawing between excitement and terror. The Japanese man meanwhile pressed his magnificent lens up against the nearest window and furiously machine-gunned the animals below with digital precision.

The radio crackled with excitement,

"Dave, Dave, there are elephant about 500 metres off your left wing!"

"Thanks Kyle." Sanders tilted the wings slightly to the left, kicked the rudder opposite and side-slipped over Kyle's tourist filled Land Rover which was also headed towards the elephant. He flew around the herd in a large gentle circle, giving his passengers as near a look as possible without causing a stampede. The animals in the reserve were used to being observed from both the air and ground and would not usually react unless approached too closely.

He circled once more and then started to climb up and away from the herds. No point in overdoing it or he would spook them and ruin Kyle's chance of giving his own passengers a good view. He flew towards the perimeter fence with the intention of following it back to the river and then up to the dam. Almost at the fence something caught his eye on the ground below. He came around lower for a second look. Satisfied he resumed the original course and thumbed the radio microphone,

"Kyle, I just saw a break in the fence and some odd tracks. Looks like you have aliens in the reserve again. Phone it in to the cops as soon as you are back at the lodge, we are too far out to raise them on the radio."

"Sure Dave", replied Kyle.

Sanders spoke as quietly as possible but was still overheard by his passengers.

"Ariens", repeated the Japanese passenger softly to himself and then held his camera at the ready just in case. The dam appeared underneath. The plane descended towards the water and splashed into a landing. Sanders taxied towards the island, stopping as close as he deemed safe and switching off the motor. Ears accustomed to its drone now rang in the silence. As normal hearing returned a quieter motor could be heard approaching. A small boat had put out from the island in order to fetch the plane's passengers and ferry them to the picnic lunch that was laid out and waiting.

Once the passengers were unloaded and the boat had left Sanders re-started the motor and eased the plane across the water towards the jetty. He tied up at the small floating raft that was anchored to the bottom of the dam by a strong steel cable. Morris arrived within a few minutes, alone in his small boat,

"Any more passengers?"

"No Sir."

"OK, take me back with you then, I'll wait at the office and see if anyone arrives soon. If not we'll call it a day."

Inside the tiny ticket-office Sanders attempted to make himself comfortable in a rickety chair and made small talk with the attendant.

"How was the flight Dave."

"Good, saw lots of game. Got in nice and close to some ellies as well. On the way back I saw a fence-break and some tracks."

"Border crossing?"

"I think so, more illegal aliens. That's what you get for being so close the Zimbabwean border hey. With the situation there a bunch of them come across almost every day."

"Can't really blame them Dave, sure it's not fun living there now."

"No you can't. Doesn't make our job any easier though. Every time they cut the bloody fence we run the risk of some animals escaping. OK if it's just a couple of buck, they're easy enough to round up. But the day a leopard or lion or something gets out and eats one of the locals there'll be hell to pay."

The rest of Saturday slipped by peacefully. Sundowners were served on the wooden deck overlooking the waterhole or around the pool where some of the guests swam or simply sat happily immersed in the cool water. Little of any great interest occurred until dinnertime.

There was mild amusement at a few neighbouring tables when a waiter politely pointed out to Boet Erasmus that the starter was called basted wings, not bastard wings. The faint titter melted away into the bushveld sounds and happy eating noises.

During the meal Cherie Erasmus noticed Boet rubbing his left wrist and frowning.

"What's wrong?"

"I can't find my watch. Was sure I left it on the side of the pool when I swam just now, but it wasn't there when I got out. I checked my pockets and everywhere. Hope it comes out, I don't want to lose it."

"Why don't you ask one of them for help?" Cherie nodded towards a mixed group eating at a long table on the patio.

"What do you mean?"

"I heard from one of the staff that they are all here on some kind of new-agey psychic convention. Aren't they supposed to be able to see stuff and tell the future and things?"

"Good idea, I'll give it a try."

When the crockery had been cleared and coffee was on its way Boet stood up and headed over to the patio. From her place at the head of the table Boet rightly assumed that Claire was the leader of the group and addressed her,

"Sorry to bother you", he said, "but I heard you are a psycho." The blunt statement hung like a negative aura over the conversation at the table.

Claire staggered mentally for a few moments and then recovered with a smile,

"Oh, I think you mean psychic. Yes I am."

"I know I'm being a nuisance but I need some help."

"Can't promise anything but we'll do whatever we can to help a fellow guest."

"I lost my watch and was wondering if you or one of your friends could help me to find it. It belonged to my grandfather and I'd hate to lose it."

"I might be able to help you with that. Do you have anything with you that is usually with the watch, a case perhaps?"

"No, not with me."

"OK no problem, I'll try without it. Which hand do you wear your watch on?"

"Left."

"Sit here and give me your left hand."

Boet sat on the edge of the chair that had kindly been vacated by one of Claire's colleagues.

She placed her fingertips lightly on the pale strip of skin that indicated where the watch was usually worn and closed her eyes,

"I'm sensing darkness and warmth, like the inside of a body." She looked up confused, "Also a long neck and pebbles. That probably doesn't make much sense."

Boet sat pondering for a moment then jumped up.

" Yes it does! There were some ostriches poking their heads through the fence by the pool earlier. I chased them away by splashing some water at them.

I'll bet one of the *bliksems* took my watch and swallowed it!"

"Sounds logical. And ostriches like shiny objects don't they?"

"Yes and they swallow small stones to help them digest. Do you think you could help me tell which ostrich it was?"

"Possibly, but it's very dark now and will be difficult to find them. Meet me here after breakfast and I'll see what I can do for you. Maybe we can ask one of the rangers to find the ostriches for us and get us close to them. I might be able to sense which one has your watch."

"Thank you so much Miss…?"

"Voyant, but please call me Claire."

Boet returned to his table a lot happier than he had left it. At least he had a plan and some chance of getting his watch back.

Sunday morning dawned grey and overcast. Boet was up early, impatient to get on with the business of finding his watch. He fidgeted through breakfast, which Cherie and he had almost finished by the time most of the guests were beginning theirs. He spotted Claire and waved. She came over to the table,

"Don't worry, I haven't forgotten my promise. I'll help you as soon as we've eaten."

"Thank you."

Claire and her group moved away to their table. Boet went to the reception counter to see if he could arrange to speak to one of the game rangers about locating the ostriches.

The attractive young lady at the front desk was very helpful and called her duty manager. The manager listened to the request and explanation with patience then promised to see what he could do. He disappeared back into the office to contact the head ranger for assistance.

Within a few minutes he was back. "I'm afraid I have a bit of bad news sir. Someone cut a hole in our perimeter fence within the last day or so, we suspect it was illegal aliens crossing from Zimbabwe. Early this morning one of our rangers on patrol discovered that some of the ostriches had escaped through the hole. A team of rangers is about to leave to try round them up, they are just calling the police first for some assistance."

Boet's face tumbled in despair. Now what? He was however a man of action and didn't let this obstacle stand in his way for long. As he rushed off to make some alternative plans the telephone call mentioned by the duty manager took place between the ranger's office and the front desk of the local police station,

"We have an ostrich situation here. A few of them escaped through a hole made by Zim refugees and are running around in a panicked state outside. Need some help to close the road before someone gets hurt."

An acknowledgement came from the other end of the line.

" OK, got it. You have some hosstriches on the loose. Let me see what I can do. I'll call you back."

Sergeant Bobby Naaidoo put down the telephone handset, deciding that he should talk to his superior immediately. He approached the station commander's office with trepidation. Lieutenant Sybrand Van Niekerk could be a fearsome character and was not known for his patience with subordinates.

"Ja. What is it?" he yelled in answer to the enquiring knock. Bobby opened the door and approached with caution.

"Naaidoo! What do you want, I'm busy"

The magazine open on the desk seemed to disagree with this statement, but Bobby was not going to be the one to point this out.

"Sir, I just had a radio call from the game reserve. They hare hasking for some elp."

A quaver of fear overlaid his characteristic Durban Indian accent, common to many in his community of South Africans of Indian descent.

"What sort of help?"

"They want us to close the road in front of the lodge, they ave a situation with one hosstrich and hare hafraid someone will get urt."

Van Niekerk sat bolt upright.

"A hostage situation!"

"Hosstrich, Sir."

"That's what I said. We better scramble a task team."

"You sure that's necessary sir?"

"Don't question me Naaidoo!" thundered Van Niekerk. "I'll decide what's necessary. You get back to the rangers and tell them I'm handling the situation and will get some help out there."

Bobby returned to the front desk with the feeling that the situation had been misunderstood. This frequently happened due to his accent and that of his Afrikaner superior being only semi-intelligible to each other. He suddenly felt more homesick than usual for his far-away coastal home town.

Still fresh in his mind was the incident when he had sent a patrol vehicle out to check on a report from a local about a group of strangers gathering in a field near the town. The report came back that all was well, it was only a group of writers engaging in an exercise to "unclutter their minds". Odd as this seemed to the local rural population it was not dangerous and as no laws were being broken, or even slightly damaged, he took no action.

His superior however, who had heard snatches of the radio conversation through his open office door, was not as passive. Newly promoted, he was keen to make a name for himself and move from being a small-town station commander to a more prestigious post elsewhere.

Within a short space of time some local residents were treated to the sight of an armoured police vehicle skidding to a halt just outside the town. A squad of large officers in riot gear charged into the field to be met by a terrified group of people, most of whom dropped their notebooks and pens in fright. Van Niekerk had a fairly difficult time explaining to both the riot unit commander and his area commissioner that it was a simple mistake and that rioter and writer really did sound very similar over the radio.

An ominous sense of déjà vu spread over Bobby Naaidoo. There was no love lost between him and the station commander though. He was of the opinion that if the great Lieutenant Van Niekerk insisted on appointing himself the village idiot, who was a lowly desk-sergeant to stand in his way. He notified the rangers that the station commander had taken control of the situation and help would be provided soon. The rangers piled into several Land Rovers and headed for the break in the fence. Boet followed at a distance in his own vehicle.

Rumours, as they generally do, spread quickly through the lodge. The duty manager had to answer a few questions and gently squash the speculation that some evidence of extra-terrestrial activity had been discovered in the reserve. One guest even reported that he had seen the rangers loading large nets, dart guns and hunting rifles into their vehicles. His widely-shared opinion was that they were off to try and capture some non-human life forms.

The rangers passed through the main gate and onto the road that ran along the outside of the perimeter fence. Boet stopped his car near the gate and watched from a distance. The man who had spotted the break and then remained to guard it waved the other rangers down. He reported that he had seen ostriches come tentatively out of the bush a few times, but they were spooked either by his presence or passing cars.

Wayne Rodgers, the head ranger, quickly arranged his staff into two teams. The first team walked about a kilometre into the open land away from the lodge fence. They then stopped and formed a line that fanned out parallel to the fence and started moving back towards the road beating sticks together and shouting. In the meantime the second team unloaded various bits of equipment to help in the capture of the ostriches.

The team of beaters moved slowly towards the road while the other team stood ready to capture any ostriches that fled in their direction. Eventually they reached the road having flushed nothing but a few indignant guinea fowl from the bushes. Rodgers glared at the veld,

"Damn, they must be further out than we thought. We could be tramping around here all day and never find them,"See if you can raise David Sanders on the radio. Maybe he can use that flying dinghy thing of his to spot them from above."

"I can't see anything from this height. Going to go around again lower, maybe the noise will scare them into the open a bit and we can get a fix on their location", said Sanders over the radio. He banked the plane around and went in again as low and slow as he dared, hoping to flush any hidden ostriches towards the road to make capture easier. The plane roared over the bushes leaving a fluttering cloud of dry leaves and dust behind. As Sanders pulled up and missed hitting the game fence by centimetres a movement on the ground tugged at the corner of his eye. He allowed the plane to drift into a lazy circle so he could determine the source of the movement.

Three human forms ran out of the dust cloud, arms raised and faces clouded with panic. Two of the rangers near the road noticed them and brought rifles up in warning. Sanders did not see what happened next as he was banking away. The rangers yelled at the men to stop or risk being shot. Compliance was immediate and they stood in terror with chests heaving and eyes wide. Rodgers snorted in disgust. He wanted his ostriches back, not more damn refugees! He looked up and watched Sanders' plane skimming over a nearby ridge. Suddenly the nose dipped, the motor gunned and the plane tore away low to the ground. Sanders must have seen something. He was about to order two of his rangers to take a Land Rover and head towards the ridge when the radio hissed to life. Sanders' voice rang out in a burst of static and urgency,

"Guys, I'm not sure what is going on here! There's a bunch of armed men lying just over the ridge watching the road with binoculars. Looks like they may be cops of some sort."

Up on the ridge Captain Peterson, the task unit commander, was in a state of confusion. Acting on information received from the local station commander the task team had raced from their home base, arriving in just under an hour. Wary of entering an unknown situation blind Peterson had consulted with Lieutenant Van Niekerk, who insisted on being involved, as to the approximate location of the reported situation. He plotted the reserve main gate as a reference point on his hand-held GPS device and then worked out a route which would bring him to the top of a ridge overlooking the road.

He took two snipers, two regular members and a radio operator with him and began working his way over the dirt roads to approach the ridge from the opposite side as the reserve. The rest of his team he left under the control of his second in command, Lieutenant Modise, with orders to approach the activity as close as was safe and to stay well concealed. He would give further orders by radio once the situation could be further assessed from the ridge.

Van Niekerk had initially insisted on going to the top of the ridge but had been told by Peterson to remain with Modise's team and stay out of the way. His objections had been firmly declined and as he was out-ranked he had no choice but to comply, muttering off in their wake and thinking ugly thoughts about cocky task team commanders.

Peterson and his team inched forward on their stomachs until they could peer over the edge of the low cliff at the top of the ridge. Nothing much appeared to be happening below. A few khaki-clad men stood around peering into the bush. He decided to wait for a bit and see if anything developed. Maybe Van Niekerk had sent them on a wild goose chase. He certainly didn't seem like the smartest cop Peterson had ever met, all bluster and arrogance with very little substance. After a short wait a small plane droned into view, circling over the area. Peterson was now even more confused. The plane was an unexpected development. Perhaps the hostage takers intended to use it to make an escape. He whispered instructions to his radio operator who worked his way backwards and slipped below the ridge before speaking, just in case his voice carried to those below.

The plane went in again, lower than before. There was something nagging at the back of Peterson's mind, a feeling that there was something odd about the plane. He couldn't quite define what it was. Whoever the pilot was he was either really good at low flying or crazy or maybe both. Height was a bit difficult to judge from above but the dust cloud and flattened grass showed that the plane was very close to the ground. Peterson stiffened as the saw the three men bolt out of the long grass. The raised rifles of the rangers shook him into action. First the presence of the plane and now an open show of weapons, something was definitely going on.

He was mentally finalising his plan of action when the plane banked away from the activity below and roared up over the ridge. Instinctively he rolled onto his back, service pistol trained on the underside of the fuselage. A large shadow swept over the men and then all that was left was dust and fluttering leaves. The tail fin receded into the distance and suddenly it dawned on Peterson. The plane was fitted with floats for water landings, making it impossible for the pilot to land and help with a getaway. This situation was far from simple. He turned back to see what was happening below. Almost all of the men were now staring up at the ridge, besides the two that still had rifles trained on their prisoners.

Peterson grabbed the radio handset. He gave rapid instructions to the team on lower ground for an encircling operation to prevent anyone from leaving the area. He stressed that they were not to approach too close or initiate any kind of contact until he arrived. He left the two snipers carefully positioned and rushed the rest of his team back to the vehicle.

The element of surprise had been lost so this time there was no need for excessive stealth. He hurled the big SUV down the dirt roads and skidded to a stop next to his 2IC.

"Anything happening?"

"Not really. They are basically just standing around staring at the ridge and the one who seems to be in charge uses some sort of radio every now and then. I think he's talking to the plane. We've seen it circle around a few times but seems to be keeping well away for now."

"Any idea who they might be or what they want? Seems a weird place to be taking hostages."

"Judging by the clothing and the vehicles they look like game rangers."

"Could be a disguise to blend in. Why would game rangers be taking hostages?"

From his vantage point in the shadow of the gate Boet watched the activity in disbelief. There appeared to be a stand off between the rangers and a group of policemen, heavily armed and in what looked like riot gear.

"Right", said Peterson. "Not much point in standing around here all day. Let's force the issue a bit." He reached into the back of his vehicle and produced a large megaphone. "Cover me; I need to talk to them." This said he stepped into the road and thumbed one of the switches. A siren sound cut briefly through the rapidly heating air. Satisfied that all eyes were now on him, he pushed another button and lifted the device to his mouth,

"I am Captain Petersen, the commander of a special task unit of the South African Police Service. We need to talk and find out what it is you want."

Rodgers almost burst out laughing. The sight of a heavily armed team of policemen standing on a secondary road in the middle of nowhere was ludicrous. How on earth did they get mixed up in a routine game capture operation? Peterson spoke again,

"I have on my team a trained negotiator. He would like to talk to a representative from your group. I will send him forward halfway to your position. He will be unarmed. Please send an unarmed man to meet him. There are two highly trained snipers on the ridge to ensure his safety but you have my assurance that they will not act against you without provocation. We don't want anyone to get hurt, just to find a way to resolve this situation."

He dropped the heavy instrument to his side and licked his lips. The loud and carefully pronounced speech had left a layer of wool on his tongue. His negotiator, a youngish blonde sergeant, began moving down the road. He walked carefully with hands held away from his body to show he was not holding a weapon.

"Let me go and see what the sundance kid here wants", muttered Rodgers. The two met midway between their respective positions. The policeman spoke first.

"We need to know what your grievance is and what your demands are. Then we may be able to find some common ground and resolve this situation peacefully."

Rodgers rolled eyes and forced smile oozed sarcasm,

"I'm not sure what situation you are referring to, but my only grievance is that you are keeping me from my work."

"The situation with the three men you are holding hostage over there." The sergeant pointed at the three dusty souls who were still being guarded by the rifle-wielding rangers.

This time Rodgers did actually laugh out loud.

"Oh them. They're not hostages. In fact I'm not quite sure where exactly they came from. We were trying to flush out some ostriches when they came running out with their hands up. Suspect they are illegals from Zim that cut the bloody hole in the fence and let the ostriches out in the first place."

"So you are not holding them hostage to make demands then."

"Hell no, you can have them if you want. I certainly have no use for them. Not like the tourists are likely to pay good money to look at them. We are from the game reserve over there. All I want is my ostriches back."

"Wait here. I need to consult with my commander." The policeman walked back and held a hurried conversation with Peters then returned,

"My commander would like to know if there is a way for us to verify your explanation."

"You mean the uniforms and Land Rovers aren't convincing enough. Hold on, I'll give you a business card and you can phone the lodge. Just make sure your snipers don't think I'm about to beat you to death with my wallet."

He reached carefully into his pocket, located the wallet and removed a card. The policeman returned to Peterson who used his cellphone to call and verify that a team had indeed been sent out to round up some ostriches.

This time Peterson himself walked down the road. He stopped, smiled and extended his hand,

"Captain Peterson. And you are Mr?"

"Wayne Rodgers."

"I'm terribly sorry about all this. It seems our

intelligence was incorrect." He glared over his shoulder in the direction of Van Niekerk who was standing in a pool of discomfort near the police vehicles.

"If he's your intelligence I'm not bloody surprised. Not the brightest boy I've ever met."

"Well I apologise Sir, we will investigate how all this happened."

"No problem, now can I get back to finding my ostriches?"

"Certainly. In fact maybe we can help. My snipers up there have infra-red binoculars that should be able to see any living thing around here. Come with me." Peterson radioed instructions to his snipers to secure their weapons and then to sweep the countryside for any sign of animals. Within a few minutes they were reporting some movement halfway up a nearby slope that could well be ostriches.

"Thanks", called Rodgers as he ran for his own vehicle. He briefly explained over the radio to Sanders what had happened and asked him to fly low over the slope to try and scare the ostriches into the open.

Sanders complied and came droning over the ridge, preparing to fly down the slope towards the road. As he tilted the nose into a shallow dive something hurtled across in front of his windscreen. He swore and instinctively pulled the stick back and to one side. The plane curved up and into a banked turn, the single propeller whining.

Sanders looked around to determine what had nearly collided with him, if it was a bird it was a huge one! He nearly choked when he saw a Rooivalk helicopter gunship tailing him and mirroring his every move. The sleek craft bristled with weapons and menace. What on earth were the air force boys doing out here and why had they buzzed him? He swung into a gentle circle to see what would happen next. He had no access to military frequencies so radio communication was out of the question.

The Rooivalk pilot made the next move. Using the impressive acceleration of his craft he cut across the circle and flew just inside and level with Sanders. The weapons systems officer, sitting in front of and slightly below the pilot, pointed down several times at the road in an obvious instruction to land.

Sanders opened his small side window and pointed carefully at the floats mounted in place of wheels. The Rooivalk crew understood. A road landing was out of the question. Sanders made a signal to indicate that they should follow him and headed for the lake.

Back at the gate Boet's eyes threatened to escape from his face. All he wanted was his watch back but it looked as if he was about to end up in the middle of a mini war. He decided that hanging around in the hope of spotting the ostrich was less important than his personal safety and drove off in the direction of the lodge, glancing in his mirror every few seconds.

He walked through the reception area, confused and despondent.

"Mr Erasmus." He turned.

"I heard you lost a watch, could this possibly be it?" The contents of the cellophane zipper bag that the receptionist held up brought a smile to his face.

"My watch! Where did you get it? I thought one of the ostriches had swallowed it."

"One of them did, or at least tried to. After one of the rangers on foot patrol reported the hole in the fence he carried on checking the area for a bit and found one ostrich lying on the ground, almost dead. He noticed a bulge in its throat and thought it may have choked so he put his fingers down its throat and found this. As soon as he pulled it out the ostrich started recovering”

"Wow, that’s amazing. Bet from now on it’ll, um, watch what it eats.”

Jackpot

Six million. Six Million!

Tom could not get the number out of his head.

His problems were over. He could settle all of his debt, buy a new house and car and invest the rest. They would never have to struggle financially ever again. They could have a lifestyle they had only ever dreamed of.

But his problems were not over, they were only beginning. Now he faced the problem of how to tell his wife. Jenny had made it abundantly clear on many occasions that she did not approve of the lottery. She regarded it as a state sponsored way to rip off poor and struggling people.

Sporadic press articles reporting how little of the money collected was actually finding its way to the supposed charitable beneficiaries rather than administrators and politicians with deep pockets only served to reinforce her opposition.

Whenever Tom mused out loud how nice it would be to win a lot of money Jenny was quick to voice her opinion that money not earned through hard work was not worth having. She was always pointing out that wealth gained suddenly would not make him happy.

Secretly Tom thought that being poor was not a guaranteed pathway to happiness either. Besides if he were going to be unhappy, he would rather be rich and unhappy than poor and unhappy. His current life was not exactly filled with ecstasy.

Winding his way home Tom still could not decide how to tell Jenny that he had won the six million midweek lottery. He was not sure if she would be happy or insist that he refuse to claim the prize. He suspected the latter.

After some soul searching and not wanting to introduce a wild card into an already problematic marriage, Tom decided not to tell Jenny just yet. He would wait until the prize money was paid out to him and then decide what to do.

The following day Tom went out in his lunchtime to fill in the official claim form at the lottery administrator's office. They explained to him that he had the right to remain anonymous if he so chose.

This was an option that he exercised, not wanting to attract a flood of distant relatives and long lost friends to his front door.

He would have a difficult enough time explaining to Jenny why he had been playing the lottery behind her back for the last eight years without having to also account for a stream of gold-diggers besieging their home.

It was also explained to him that he would be paid a lump sum equal to 20% of the winnings within the next few days. The balance would be paid out in equal instalments over the next five years. This was done to ensure that even if winners blew the initial payment with reckless spending, they would not be left destitute.

A plan began to form in Tom's mind as he returned to work. Over the next few days he opened a new account at a different bank to the one at which his regular account was held. He also rented a post office box to which all bank correspondence would be addressed.

He did this because he knew that Jenny would pick up the lump sum payment into his bank account. Opening his mail before he had even seen it was one of the little ways that Jenny made him feel worthless and disrespected. She checked his bank statement meticulously every month as if to catch him spending money without her prior approval.

His plan was to keep the lump sum in the new account and use part of it to settle some debts. He had incurred debts that Jenny did not even know about. Due to his low salary he had often had to borrow money to pay for groceries and other household requirements.

He had avoided telling his wife about these debts out of fear that she would ridicule him again over his inability to get a better paying job. While he was making arrangements to pay the amounts concerned the rest of his plan unfolded in his mind.

He did two more things. He notified his employer that he would be leaving at the end of the month then went out and bought a new suit which he kept hidden at work until needed.

When he arrived at home that evening he told the first lie to his wife.

"Jenny, guess what."

"What?"

"I was offered a better job today"

"Where?"

"At a new stationary wholesaler that has opened up across town."

"Doing what?"

"I will be a sales representative. The salary is much better than what I'm getting now. The only downside is that I will be on the road all day calling on clients. I might even have to stay away from home one or two nights a month."

As he said this last sentence Tom secretly thought that this was one of the best parts of his plan. A few nights away from home occasionally would at least keep him sane.

"What makes you think you can be a sales rep? Just because you've been an orders clerk for eight years doesn't necessarily mean that you have the ability to take on more responsibility"

"Well they think I can do it. As a matter of fact I have already accepted the position."

The uncharacteristic defiance in Tom's voice seemed to annoy Jenny.

"Well as long as you don't get fired after a few months. We have bills to pay you know."

The end of the month approached. Tom enjoyed his last few days of work more than any other, except maybe the first few. He had been young, energetic and eager to please. Now he was a little older, tired and eager to leave.

His job had become simply something to do every day, an exercise in futility tolerated only for financial reasons. He had realised early on that he did not have what it takes to be a success in the corporate world.

He did not have the drive, ambition or killer instinct to make it to the top. He also did not have the arrogance, greed and disregard for peoples dignity that was evident in the upper echelons of the company he worked for. He had neither the ability nor the inclination to be a successful corporate type.

Days trickled into weeks, weeks evolved into months, months morphed into years. Tom worked, he observed, he dreamed. Through all the years he played the lottery faithfully every week, at first openly and later surreptitiously having been the whipping boy of Jenny's disapproval on several occasions.

The slight defiance which playing the lottery in secret allowed him to feel lent a little excitement to his life, a single ray of beaming warmth through cold grey skies.

The last hour of the last day of Tom's job came to an end. He smiled and shook hands politely at the few well-wishers who gathered at his desk and left as he had come, quietly and unobtrusively.

The next day he left the house as usual except for the new suit he was wearing.

"Are you sure we can afford a new suit?" Jenny said sharply when he brought it home.

I don't know if "we" can afford it but "I" certainly can, thought Tom. Aloud he said,

"It's expected of me to dress better now that I am representing the company in public. Besides the extra money I will be making will more than cover the cost."

He spent the day driving around aimlessly revelling in being able to simply waste time, his time. Jenny could not take away from him the freedom of those few hours and he did not have to account for his time to a boss.

This he did everyday for the next two months, sometimes driving in the country, sometimes going down to the beach, always doing whatever he felt like. On the last day of each month he dutifully transferred a sum equal to his new "salary" from the account holding his winnings to his regular account.

In the third month he grew bolder and made two overnight "business trips". The freedom of a night's peace in a hotel full of strangers was indescribable.

In the sixth month he came home driving a new car. A company car, he explained to Jenny, allocated to him as a result of all the good work he had been doing. She seemed pleased, though whether because of his success or because she now had the use of his old car Tom could not be sure. He chuckled to himself as he remembered the look on the salesman's face when he found out that Tom would be paying cash for his brand new car and not financing it with a loan.

The months stretched on. Tom and Jenny continued to live their lives, joined but separate. The business trips grew longer and more frequent. Jenny's response each time grew colder.

Tom continued to live in his fantasy world, every now and then awarding himself a slight salary increase. Jenny almost never asked about his work or what he had done during the day. This was not entirely unusual, as she had seldom enquired when Tom actually had a job. They lived together in relative peace and harmony but with no real affection. Tom brought money into the home and Jenny spent it.

Occasionally he wondered what it would have been like had he felt free to tell Jenny the truth. They could have lived like kings on the winnings. He stopped short of telling the truth because he could never be sure if this revelation would heal their marriage or destroy it forever. He was not prepared to take the risk. Even though they had a far from perfect relationship, it gave some stability to his life to be able to come home to Jenny whenever he chose.

One ordinary day the situation changed irrevocably. Tom pulled into the driveway and noticed Jenny's car was not there. Strange, she had never been away when he arrived home before. He entered the house and felt immediately that something was different but could not define exactly what it was. Looking around the lounge it struck him. The whole collection of small ceramic ornaments that Jenny had collected over the years was gone. He stared at the bare spaces on top of furniture and shelves, the vacant surfaces felt like a silent accusation.

He hurried through to the bedroom and opened the wardrobe. All of Jenny's clothes were gone. He walked back through the house to the kitchen hoping to find a note of explanation somewhere. None was visible.

Stunned, he walked out into the garden to clear his head. It was a few minutes before he noticed the sympathetic face of the woman next door peering over the hedge at him.

"Hi Tom, you alright?"

"Hi Martha. Not really. Jenny's not here and all her things are gone."

"I know. I saw her leave."

"Did she say why?"

"No, she didn't even speak to me. But I do know why."

She saw the anguished look on Tom's face and continued gently,

"She's run away with Mike from down the street, you know, the widower."

"Why?"

"I hate to be the one to tell you this, but she's been sneaking over there a lot during the day for the last few months."

"I don't believe it, Jenny was cheating on me?"

"I'm afraid so. As soon as she found out this morning that he had won a whole lot of money playing poker she packed her bags and they disappeared."

Suspicious Behaviour

"What's that?"

"Where?"

"Over there. There's some sort of flashing light. May be a signal to somebody."

Lieutenant Johnny Delport, Alpha Team leader, looked again through his binoculars to verify his first impression. Satisfied that it was not just his imagination he said,

"Take a line from us to John Ross House, there's a long low block of flats about 500 metres to the left. Second window from the left side, I'd say fourth or fifth floor."

"Got it", confirmed Bernie Williams. As the senior customs agent on the joint police / customs task unit that was currently investigating the entry of suspected contraband cigarettes to South Africa via Durban Harbour he worked very closely with Johnny. Their intelligence so far indicated that the cigarettes were of Zimbabwean origin and were being moved overland through Mozambique to the coast north-east of the South African border. From there they suspected that the contraband was being sneaked in via fishing boats that regularly entered and exited the harbour, often in the middle of the night.

Pirating of big international brands with cheaply and illegally produced cigarettes made from local tobacco was becoming commonplace and a headache for both law enforcement agencies and the health authorities. The finished product was increasingly to be seen on sale at street corners and flea markets all over South Africa.

"Wonder what it means?" said Bernie.

"Or who it is meant for?" replied Johnny, "No sign of anyone besides us out here tonight." This was the seventh consecutive night they had spent observing from the pitching and rolling deck of the small cabin cruiser. Plain clothes policemen had also been deployed at strategic points along the dockside where the fishing boats usually offloaded their catch. Absolutely no sign of any contraband had been reported.

Judging by the amount of product on the streets it was coming in regularly but they were never able to locate the source. Their suspicion now was that there was someone stationed nearby on land or possibly another boat that was aware of the movements of the police and customs officials.

The task team had spent their nights hoping to spot one of the incoming boats or their land-based accomplices. Finally it looked as if they had a lead. Johnny turned away from the handrail and called softly for one of his team to join him. A young policeman approached. Johnny handed him the binoculars and briefly explained the situation then stepped back. Williams moved back and joined him.

"This youngster is a communications and encryption specialist. He's very sharp and also has a good knowledge of Morse code", explained Johnny.

Williams nodded at the clarification and said,

"Hopefully he can give us out first real clue."

"I hope so too."

The young officer approached them, notebook in hand and looking puzzled.

"Get anything?" asked Johnny.

"Sort of sir. Definitely looks like a light being used to send info in Morse code, but I can't make any sense of it."

Why not?" As he snapped the question Johnny regretted it. They were all on edge and it wasn't the youngster's fault.

"If it is a signal it's in a foreign language. Here's all I managed to get before it stopped." He handed the notebook to Johnny.

Fydor nersk zng fokov

"Hmm", said Johnny. "Not a whole lot of help."

"Looks like it may be Russian or something", chipped in Williams over Johnny's shoulder.

"Hmm", said Johnny again. "Maybe there's some foreign involvement here. Some people in Mozambique are still very cosy with their old Russian allies."

He ducked into the boat's cabin and radioed back to their home base. He first reported on what had been seen, with an approximate location of the window from which the signal came. The operator confirmed that Bravo team would be sent out to investigate. Johnny's request to locate someone who understood Russian was met with some hesitation and followed by a weak promise to see what could be arranged.

He told the operator to get the Bravo team leader to make contact with him once they were in position near the block of flats and he would do his best to guide them to the correct unit.

While he waited Johnny sat in the bow of the craft with his feet propped up on the stainless steel guard rail. The distant lights rose and fell in and out of view in time with the gently heaving swell. From this distance the Victoria Embankment had a magical look about it, all twinkling lights and impressive architecture.

Johnny knew well enough though that the reality was far different. In recent years the drug dealing and prostitution that had always existed on the point had steadily spread outwards, swallowing the embankment and spitting out filth. It made an awkward neighbour to the many elderly people who inhabited the flats. Most had retired there in order to enjoy the sea air and view of the yachts in the nearby marina.

The radio came to life with a burst of static. Bravo team was in position and awaiting instructions. Johnny walked to the side rail where the young officer was keeping watch through the binoculars.

"Anything?"

"Not really sir. The odd short flash, but nothing that could be decoded."

"OK, let's try to get an accurate fix on the location and send Bravo Team in to check it out."

Inside the flat Mrs Maureen Madsen was fast approaching insanity. The blinds that her son had fitted for her over the weekend just would not co-operate. It had seemed like a good idea at the time to replace the ageing curtains with nice modern Italian-looking blinds, but the fiddly mechanisms and cords that tangled at will were now working on her nerves. The several large G&T's which she had poured to calm herself only made matters worse. As the evening wore on the ratio of G to T steadily swung in favour of G.

The resulting effect was that she was now not only angry but also rather unsteady and in even less of a position to work out where the problem lay. The more agitated she became the more she drank, the more she drank the less likely she was to untangle the cords. The situation degenerated into a vicious circle of alcohol and rage. Exasperated she rattled the blinds furiously; hoping to cure by brute force what she could not by patience and dexterity.

On the boat the young communications expert was gently rocking with the tide and observing idly through the binoculars. Suddenly he stiffened as wild flashes of light emanated from the flat window.

Within seconds Inspector Johnny Delport was at his side.

"Get any of that?"

"No sir, it was too fast and erratic. If they are signalling someone he must be really good with Morse to be able to decode that."

"At least we've got a good clear fix on the location this time. I managed to take a photo during that last lot of flashing."

Johnny ducked into the cabin and connected the digital camera to his laptop computer. He uploaded the photo and used imaging software to enlarge a section of the picture. Now he could clearly identify the window from which the signal came and could even see a dark figure stooped behind the bright flare of light.

Maureen was sitting glaring at the blinds when she heard the thud of multiple booted feet in the passage outside. There was a silent pause before the door exploded off its hinges and landed untidily on the fake Persian rug in the entrance hall. Several large men wearing bullet-proof vests and severe expressions spilled into the room through the cloud of dust left by the falling door.

A red dot of light swept across the floor then upwards and affixed itself to the centre of her forehead.

"Don't move! Raise your hands slowly and keep them raised."

The thought crossed Maureen's mind that it would

be hard to raise her hands without moving at all. She decided though that debating logical semantics with a group of heavily armed men would not be sensible and did as she was told. The team leader stared at Maureen with confused suspicion. She didn't look like a Russian smuggler, but then again it could be a clever disguise.

Two of the team members swept through the small flat looking in all the rooms and then reported that they had seen nothing suspicious. The team leader decided they must have the wrong flat and gave the order to withdraw. The team stormed out of the flat in a flurry of embarrassment. As they fled the leader called for urgent support from the quartermaster's division. He also left one of his men in the passage near Maureen's flat to keep watch while the door was out of order.

Maureen sank into a chair and sat in a shocked state contemplating her empty doorway. She couldn't decide if the events of the last few minutes were real or just a gin-induced hallucination. She almost hoped the latter. She sat in this state for a while. Eventually the shock wore off and she became progressively angrier as she stared at the door, lying out of its natural element on the floor. After about 30 minutes had passed she again heard the sound of boots in the passage.

The team leader stepped through the door and timidly addressed Maureen,

"Hello ma'am. We are back to attend to some unfinished business. My apologies. We had intelligence that someone was using this flat to send signals to smugglers, it appears the information was inaccurate."

Maureen was about to make a comment about the wisdom of the term intelligence in the current context but decided that sarcasm would be as bad an idea as debating semantics. Instead she said,

"Well young man I assure you that I'm no smuggler, nor do I know any! Now just what are you going to do about my door?"

"We brought someone to assist with that."

The task team members stood aside to allow a colleague from QM division to enter the flat. He shook his head at the door lying prone on the carpet. After muttering something about task force bozos he opened a large toolbox and got to work. Expertly he fitted a new set of brass hinges, a lock and nice new handles. With the help of two task team members he refitted the door and screwed the hinges to the wooden frame, which fortunately had no serious damage. All that remained was to grease the hinges and touch up a few rough spots with a small brush and tin of varnish.

He was packing up his tools when he glanced around the room and noticed the blinds hanging tangled and crooked. He crossed to the window. After a few minutes expert fiddling he had them neatly arranged and responding perfectly to the cord control.

Job completed, the team leader apologised once again and then he and his people withdrew as quickly and with as much dignity as they could muster.

As they were leaving the building the team leader's radio exploded with excitement,

"Bravo leader this is alpha leader. We've just seen more light signals. Acknowledge urgent over…"

The Plot

"Oh no", thought Ken, "There's that motor-mouth Clive."

Clive was one of the few colleagues with whom Ken did not get along well. His sheer arrogance and relentless sales pitching, even when away from the office, were overpowering. Silently hoping that Clive would not notice him Ken slipped into one of the folding chairs near the back of the room.

He was disappointed. Clive stood on one side of the room, rotating slowly and looking up and down the rows of chairs. His gaze landed on Ken he so he grinned and called out,

"Kenny, Howzit." He swaggered across the room and hurled himself into the empty chair next to Ken.

"Mind if I sit here?" he asked, rhetorically since he was already seated.

Actually Ken did mind. He minded having his personal space invaded, he minded being forced to spend time with Clive and most of all, he minded being called "Kenny".

He would much rather have been left alone to concentrate on the development launch due to start in a few minutes. However he was not the type to complain or be rude. He merely acknowledged Clive vaguely and concentrated on reading the promotional material that he had been handed at the door.

A man, who appeared to be in charge of the launch, stepped up to the lectern at the front of the room, switched on the microphone and began speaking,

"Ladies and Gentlemen! Welcome to the

opportunity of a lifetime. Pay careful attention. You will probably never have another opportunity like the one before you today."

As he continued, Ken began to develop a dislike for the speaker. He found the presentation very long on hype and very short on detail. There were plenty of artist's impressions of what the security village should look like; all model couples, towering mansions and sparkling swimming pools.

Optimistic figures regarding the value-growth potential of the currently undeveloped area were given as the major reason why the audience should immediately purchase plots in the new development.

The information seemed to Ken altogether too focused on the financial aspect, with no real discussion of the lifestyle requirements of the audience. He found this method of marketing too pressured and distasteful, if not downright dishonest. Actually the speaker reminded him a lot of Clive. The presentation ended and a group of people began to throng the front of the room, firing questions at the strategically placed agents and peering at the scale models and large maps on display.

"So what do you say, how many are you going to buy?" asked Clive.

"I don't think I want to buy any", was Ken's reply.

"Why not, it's a fantastic opportunity. The plots are cheaper than any other development in the area and property prices in Johannesburg have doubled in the last five years. How can you miss?"

With a sigh Ken gave reasons for his reservations,

"First, all we have been shown are artist's impressions and materials prepared by the developer's marketing people. There is not even an aerial photograph of the site or any real evidence that the location is as wonderful as we have been told."

"Second, no visit to the site was offered or even suggested, it could be down a dirt road and next door to a rubbish dump for all we know.

"Third, the fact that house prices have doubled in the last five years is no guarantee that they will do so in the next five. Salaries do not double every five years. Sooner or later affordability is going to put the brakes on the property boom."

"That's why you'll never be filthy rich", countered Clive, "You're too negative. I'm going to buy five."

"Five", said Ken incredulously, "What do you want with five houses?"

"Don't be *dof* man. I might build on one of them. By the time building starts all the plots will be sold and demand will have pushed the prices way up. I'll sell four of the plots for way more than I paid for them. I might even sell all five if the price is right. You watch, I'll probably double my money."

"Don't you think that's a bit risky?"

"Prices always go up and there are always buyers if you know where to look. Besides, no risk, no reward."

Clive was already on his way to the front of the room. That last remark sounded to Ken suspiciously like something Clive may have heard on radio or television. Was he really going to base his investment strategy on a second hand slogan?

As he drove home Ken was still annoyed by Clive's flippant opinions. True, the company had grown enormously over the last year resulting in each department manager earning substantial profit share bonuses, on average a little over half a million rand. Still. He could not see that buying five plots in an unknown development at R100,000 apiece was a wise way to spend the money.

Ken was sitting quietly in his office handling

paperwork the next Monday morning when he heard Clive's voice in the passage outside.

"Hey Kenny, you really missed out on Saturday. I hear they sold 75% of the plots there and then and that the rest will probably go today."

"I'm comfortable with my decision, good luck with yours."

"You'll be sorry when I'm filthy rich and you're still stuck here", laughed Clive as he walked away.

That day after work Ken decided to take a drive past the proposed site and see it for himself. It seemed a fairly decent piece of land, a bit remote perhaps but the city would catch up to it soon. The one aspect that still bothered him was the amount of empty land adjacent to the site. You could never tell what would be built next door. Squatters could move onto the land and crash the value overnight. Also the industrial area visible in the distance could be a source of noise and pollution.

He thought no more about the property until the middle of the next week when Clive abruptly burst into his office.

"Kenny my man, I need your help. I have to go through to one of my major customers in Pretoria in the next few days and I need you to come with. He has some distribution issues he needs to discuss with you. I'll buy you lunch and on the way back in we can pop in and see how my plots are doing."

Ken thought for a moment and then said,

"I'm a bit busy for the rest of the week, how about Monday morning?"

"Sounds OK, I'll meet you here at nine."

On Monday morning at nine-fifteen Clive strolled in to Ken's office. Having offered no apology for his lateness he looked at Ken and said,

"What's the matter with you, you look tired?

Rough party, too much dop over the weekend, wife wearing you out hey?"

The last question was accompanied by an exaggerated lewd wink.

"Actually if you must know I was doing some building over the weekend and I'm a bit tired and stiff."

"Hah, building", grinned Clive, "You should have bought a couple of plots while they were available. Then you could really build."

The business with the client was soon over. Most of the logistical questions were purely routine and could easily have been dealt with in a telephone call. Ken suspected that Clive was merely showing off to the customer by proving to him that he could drag the National Logistics Manager along with him if he so wished.

He also had the feeling that Clive wanted an excuse to drive past the development property to rub in the fact that he had bought plots and Ken had not.

Midway between Pretoria and Johannesburg they turned off the highway and drove a few kilometres into an as yet uninhabited area.

"Look at that view", said Clive.

Personally Ken did not find the view of the highway and the industrial area beyond particularly appealing, but he nodded and smiled anyway. The site was already walled and the temporary gates locked. Inside a crew of workers could be seen digging trenches, presumably for storm-water or sewerage pipes.

They could not gain access to the site so Clive contented himself with driving down the newly built road that ran along one side of the property.

They reached the corner of the property. The wall made a sharp left turn and continued away from the road at right angles. Clive began to turn the car around in order to head back the way they had come but stopped when Ken said abruptly,

"Hold on, what's that?"

"What's what?"

"Over there against the wall, in the dip."

"Don't know."

Clive climbed out of the car and squinted down the line of the wall. What he saw made him lose his cocky demeanour and look slightly pale.

"They look like shacks to me", observed Ken, who had also climbed out of the car.

"Probably just sheds that the builders are using."

"Why would the builders put sheds on the outside of the wall, not on the site? Are you sure those aren't squatters?"

"If they are it's only a couple, easy enough to get rid of them if they become a problem", said Clive, looking less than convinced by his own words.

"That's what they said about Zewendfontein", replied Ken climbing back into the car.

On the drive back to the office Clive was unusually silent and fidgeted constantly. Obviously the thought of the development being surrounded by squatters before he had a chance to sell his plots was weighing heavily on his mind.

Later that day Ken received a call from Mike, an old friend and more recently an estate agent.

"Hey Ken, want to buy some property? I've got some dynamite plots for you."

"Seriously?"

"Oh yes, your buddy Clive has been doing the rounds of the agencies the whole day offering five plots for sale. I called him and told him that I was very interested in buying them for myself. He wanted to sell me all five at a hundred thousand each. Then I told him that I had heard some rumours about squatters moving into the area and that I'd like to go out to the site and take a look around before committing to anything."

"What did he say?"

"He started to get a bit pushy and told me that he needed to sell urgently for personal reasons and that he had other people interested. He also told me that he would make me a special deal and give them to me for R80,000 apiece if I took all five, but he needed an answer today. He was here half an hour ago signing the papers. He's probably back in the office by now."

"I'll call you later; I want to go and accidentally bump into him and see what he says."

Ken strolled through the building looking for Clive. He found him in the kitchen area making coffee, strong black coffee.

"Hi Clive, how are you. How's the property wheeling and dealing going? Are you a billionaire yet?" asked Ken as he took a mug from the cupboard.

"Actually I sold those plots today."

"So soon, you can't have made much profit on them."

"Ja well, I decided I didn't really like the area anyway. I'll try my luck elsewhere sometime. You win some you lose some."

As Clive walked away Ken noticed that he had lost the swagger and most of the arrogance.

"Serves him right", he thought.

Later he called Mike back to thank him for the part he played in deflating Clive's ego.

"Not at all Ken, I should be thanking you. I've already found buyers for three of the plots at R120,000 each and I should be able to sell the other two in the next few days. How did Clive look?"

"Suitably broken."

"Hey listen Ken, one last thing. You and me better go back this weekend and break those shacks down again, before somebody actually does decide to move into them."

Ken agreed. It had been back breaking work, but it was worth it.

Glossary of Local and Slang Terms:

ATM	Auto Teller Machine (cash point)
Apartheid	Policy of racial segregation practiced in South Africa from 1948 to 1994
Bakkie	Light pick-up truck
Bliksem	Rascal
Bru	Literally, brother. Used as a generic form of casual address
East Rand	Area on the eastern side of Greater Johannesburg. Predominantly working class / industrial
Dof	Dull / Stupid
Dominee	Minister (religious, in the main/traditional Afrikaans churches)
Dop	Alcohol
Dronk	Drunk (Afrikaans)
Hawu	General term of amazement / exclamation (Zulu).
Ja	Yes (Afrikaans)
Lekker	Nice
Lightie	Small boy / youngster
Pap	Stiff cooked maize meal
Platteland	Rural area (Lit. flat land. So used due to most of South Africa's rural farming areas lying on the flat plateau-like hinterland.)
Skelm	Crook / criminal
Tsotsi	Young gangster
Umngqusho	Samp and beans
Veld	Open land or bush
Verkrampte	Narrow minded / intolerant

Translation of Back Cover Latin Quote:

Ex Africa semper aliquid novi – Always something new out of (from) Africa

About the Author

Darrell Cuthbert has been writing fiction for as long as he can remember. At school essays were his favourite part of the work.
This interest continued into adulthood, leading to a passion for reading, studying and writing short stories.

Darrell lives in Durban, South Africa, with his wife and two teenage children.

www.ingramcontent.com/pod-product-compliance
Lightning Source LLC
Chambersburg PA
CBHW031256060726
47590CB00003B/933